The Earl of Burton

The Earl of Burton

By
J. Robert Mathias

Introducing My Father
J Robert Mathias

E-BookTime, LLC
Montgomery, Alabama

The Earl of Burton

Copyright © 2006 by J. Robert Mathias

All rights reserved. No part of this book may be reproduced or transmitted in any form or by any means, electronic or mechanical, including photocopying, recording, or by any information storage and retrieval system, without permission in writing from the copyright owner.

ISBN: 1-59824-283-0

First Edition
Published June 2006
E-BookTime, LLC
6598 Pumpkin Road
Montgomery, AL 36108
www.e-booktime.com

Contents

Acknowledgement 7

Foreword 9
   Earl and Goldie Mathias 10
   The Hay Wagon 11
   A Map of Burton 12

CHAPTER 1 - *Who Was the "Earl" of Burton?* 13
   Dad, the Earl of Burton 15
   A Day in the Life of Earl 21
   Earl – Breeder of Belgian Draft Horses 24
   Earl, One Who Aided Animals 32
   Earl, One Who Helped People 35
   Earl During the World Wars 39
   Earl's Dog, Bill 43

CHAPTER 2 - *It Was the Worst of Times* 47
   The Great Depression 49
   The Winter Wood 55
   The Blizzard of 1926 62
   The Rains Came 69
   The Milk Strike 73

CHAPTER 3 - *Life on "Earl's" Farm* 79
   Feasting on the Farm 81
   The Cellar 90
   Wash Day 93
   Our Barn 96

Contents

CHAPTER 4 - *Special Memories of "Earl"* 99
    The Bee Tree 101
    Automobile Tales 104
    The Indianapolis Bus Barn 108
    Dexterity Too! 112
    Wawasee Revival! 115
    The Burton Church Picnic 119
    The Gypsies 125
    Crossing the Erie by a Hair 130

CHAPTER 5 - *Farming Without "Earl"* 135
    The Sermonette 137
    Neighbors 140
    Cow in the Muck! 142

From My Pen 145

Acknowledgement

My debt will never be repaid to my daughter Sheri for her assistance in creating this publication and in our old age. I must also thank my girlfriend, Lois, who is celebrating our 65th wedding anniversary with me.

Sheri and Lois, 1949

Foreword

As the author of these incidents, I wish to introduce you to my dad and the world of the 20's and 30's wherein he did a very unusual thing. He married a girl, had a family and developed a means of supporting them during a time when a series of cataclysmic impediments were confronted. The derailments were: The Great Depression, natural forces drove Calvary attacks, including a three year drought of great proportions, choking blizzards, floods and hordes of grasshoppers, locust and insects, which leveled crops. The whole country withered under this barrage and many of the farmers collapsed. There was no rescue in those years. My father too was very vulnerable, grossly in debt and had no capital to carry a large operation.

But......My dad had the indomitable will of a bulldog. His nature rejected defeat. He had at his disposal a continuous reserve of renewable energy. He could work around the clock if necessary. He refused to yield and brought his family and community through those perilous times.

Foreword

Earl and Goldie on their Wedding Day

Foreword

On the Hay Wagon: Ross daughter, Goldie (my mother) sitting in the hay, the other Ross daughter in front of Earl. The lady standing on the hay wearing the big hat was Mrs. Ross, then her friend, then my dad, Earl and his dad, elderly J.J. Mathias. On the ground 2 hay loaders and 2 of my mother's friends, being alluring to whatever was around.

In 1918 when the engagement was underway, my mother, Goldie was employed by a wealthy Rochester family as a nanny for their two daughters, ages 6 and 8. The Ross's owned a Tool and Die Works company.

Mrs. Ross, the wife was greatly interested in Goldie's engagement. It was a warm summer day. She loaded her new Oldsmobile touring car with a friend, her daughters, Goldie, and Goldie's friends. They wore dust caps and had a dust cover on their laps. Goldie directed them to the field where Earl was making hay. They surprised Earl! Mrs. Ross and her friend were the outgoing type and somehow got up on the partially loaded fresh hay and Grandma Mathias snapped Goldie's new camera and here it is.

Foreword

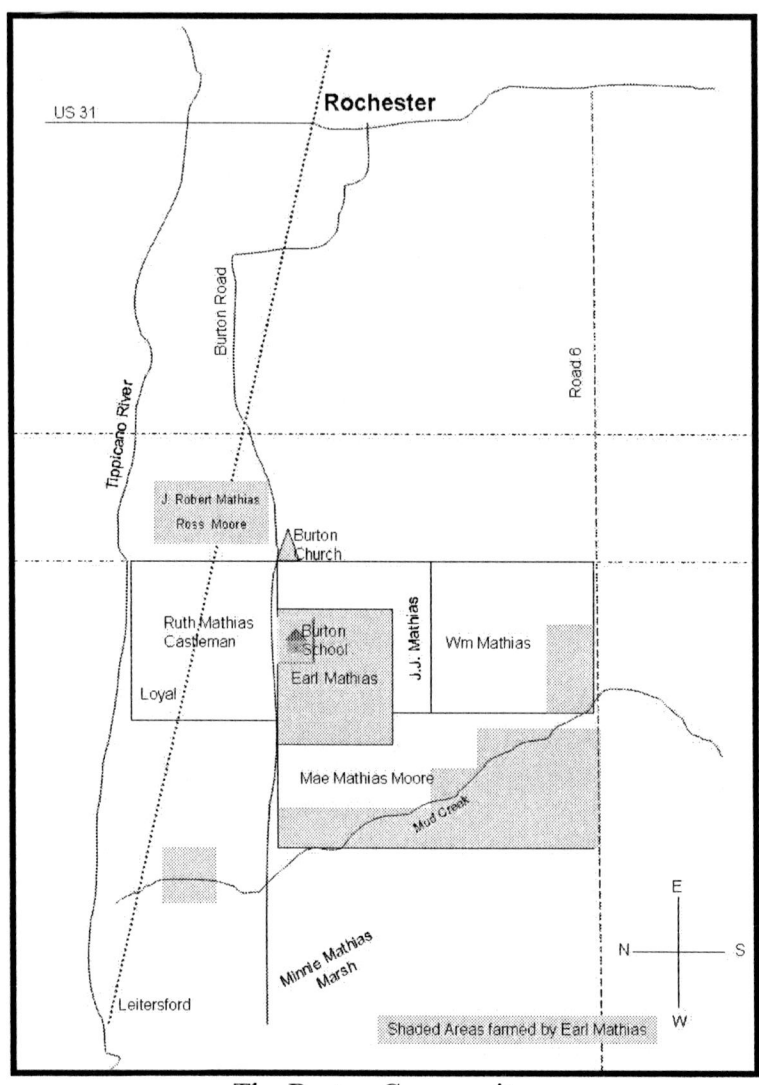

The Burton Community

CHAPTER 1

Who Was the "Earl" of Burton?

Dad, the Earl of Burton 15

A Day in the Life of Earl 21

Earl – Breeder of Belgian Draft Horses 24

Earl, One Who Aided Animals 32

Earl, One Who Helped People 35

Earl During the World Wars 39

Earl's Dog, Bill 43

Dad, the Earl of Burton

My father was a farmer, a breeder of Draft horses, a practical Veterinarian, a dairyman, a school bus driver, a singer and a good neighbor.

My dad was a worker. He rose early each day, around 4:30 a.m., and toiled rapidly and diligently all day and rarely finished to his chair before 8:00 p.m. He fed and milked 25 or more dairy cows, fed twelve horses, harnessed four or more of them, cooled his milk, drove the school bus, and was in the fields working by 8:30 a.m. At noon he would meet a farmer that had two mares to be serviced by King Albert, then back to the fields 'til 3:00 pm, when it was school bus time. Forty-five minutes later he was back in the field, moved on to an appointment with Major de Hemel to breed a mare at 6:30pm, milked the cows and fed the animals and hurried to get to supper by 8:00pm.

These daily duties were often interrupted by the need to help my mother do the heavy work of washing clothes or his passion and reputation for doing veterinarian duties for neighbors. Had he lived at a later date, he undoubtedly would have aspired to be a veterinarian, as nothing challenged him more than this work. I don't believe he was ever paid for the hundreds of hours of veterinarian work.

As a wise neighbor he was constantly interrupted to deal with all kinds of personal problems, farm problems, and even church problems. He was a ready-and-willing neighbor. These things often caused him to get behind in his own work forcing him to work harder to catch up.

He married at 24 years, purchased 120 acres, and firmly believed hard work would bring him rewards. Post World War I, farm prices were high and he paid $80,000 for the farm. It was a period of economic optimism. He had several years of good farm prices, but in 1929 the USA suffered an economic collapse. This was The Great Depression. The stock market went to the bottom. Factories and offices closed. There was wholesale loss of jobs everywhere and at all levels and kinds. Banks closed their doors. For most farm items there was no market. The Pure Milk Association continued to ship milk into Chicago, but at give-away prices.

My parents had to make an annual farm payment on December 15th and where was the big money of $9,500.00 to come from? In 1929 he managed to make it from past savings, but now should he join the other hundreds of thousands of farmers who defaulted and had their farms sold at public action? In our community several had been auctioned and the mortgage holders became the owner by default. For many it was the way to proceed, as by 1936 you could buy back the farm at a fraction of the value with subsidies, etc.

However, this did not fit my father's BULL DOG nature. He had an obligation and one way or the other he would see it through. Thus he became a breeder of horses and the driver of a school bus - it was sure money. In addition, he had several life insurance policies, which he had started before he married and whenever a farm payment was due, he took the cash value from one or more policies. Finally, the government had many public works programs to give people work and my dad hauled gravel with his team at $3.75 per day. Sometimes he would come home after a long hard day of hauling gravel, change teams, eat supper,

The Earl of Burton

milk and then take another team to plow corn or tend his crops until 11:00 at night. Today we use the word workaholic - he was a driven man, driven by our farm mortgage, and his soul was owned by Omaha Mutual Life Insurance Company, but this man was a WINNER. He made it and was debt free by 1940.

Personally, my dad was a friend to all. More than that, he was always ready to help, friend or stranger, rich or poor. He always had a savings of money, some stashed away at home and some in the bank. When the bank collapsed, he lost several hundred dollars. Money borrowers often came to him and, too often, he gave them enough to see them through. Once my cousin Paul thought he would not be able to continue law school, but Dad quickly said, "No", and he and Uncle Lloyd Castleman kept him going. Lee Moore often had to have a booster loan. Lloyd and Donna Reese were without job or sustenance. He took his school bus, moved them and their five kids to our Mud Creek Farm, where Lloyd worked for us for several years.

He never smoked nor drank. He was a real teetotaler. When he went to the store, most men bought Prince Albert and rolled their own smokes or sucked on a pipe. Not my dad. He'd buy 5 cents worth of chocolate drops or orange slices, knowing that all his kids would enjoy it. He never swore, but had a few choice words when he was angry at a horse or mare. He had the equivalent of two years of high school at Rochester Normal College. He should have had more, but he took over the farming when his father was no longer able.

He courted my mother in a buggy and the frequency of their dates was on weekend-Sunday night. Since my mother lived in Fulton, an 8½-mile distance, he would drive his horse to see her on Sunday and back home late Sunday evening. He always said the horse knew the way, so he could curl up and go to sleep until the horse stopped at the gate. He was an average farm boy with good habits and morale traits, certainly not a Romeo, as I believe my mom was his only steady girl. He lost his hair early and always said he was a bald surrey with a fringe around the edge. He never had a cavity and his teeth were pearly white.

He knew horses and spoke their language sometimes using harsh terms to set the code of discipline. The stallions rarely got out and fought each other. But when they did, only Dad could catch them and break up what could have been a fight to the death! He taught them good horse manners and punctuated them with a whip. Major de Hemel was extremely intelligent and Dad was his instructor. He stood on two hind feet, forefeet and head high in the air and held himself there. He would lay down and roll over, shake hands, run in circles on a long lead by numbers 1, 2, and 3 times or stop with whatever was called. He would stretch into a style show, setting and holding until Dad signaled.

As a practical vet, he understood the horse anatomy and medical illnesses and injuries, along with methods of correction, as well as some vets. He was good with cows and other animals, but horses were his specialization. He had some training in Chicago for Artificial Insemination and each year he impregnated several mares artificially. He was probably one of the first in Indiana to accomplish this. IF YOU NEEDED HELP, JUST CALL EARL MATHIAS, 2 SHORTS AND ONE LONG!

As a dairyman, he understood the need to develop quality milk producers, but he was limited by funds to have a super quality bull. Today it would have been accomplished by

The Earl of Burton

artificial insemination. He was a speedy milker and would milk 25 cows or so in two hours or less, about five minutes per cow. THAT IS FAST! He could milk three cows to my one.

As a school bus driver, he was very well liked. The kids considered him a friend, but he was strict and rarely had any problems.

He was a good tenor and sang in many churches. He and my mother made a good team. He couldn't accept a church invitation too far away because he had to milk at 5:00am and 6:00pm.

How was he as a husband and father? He probably was only average. I know my mother felt pressed into a yoke she could not change. Keeping up with Dad's work ethic was like lassoing a tornado. I'm afraid he often forgot the niceties, romance and a new hat perhaps. As a father he was loving, kind and proud of us. He and mother set high standards and goals with us, yet he did not deliver much of his time to us because he had little time to give!

Note 1: My father's life was cut short by cancer of the lungs at age 59. He never smoked, but he constantly handled fertilizers and pesticides when the danger was not understood. He ate gobs of dust and dirt walking behind horse-drawn implements and riding tractors later. He was a victim of environmental abuse.

Note 2: Dad was a determined Republican and followed in the steps of his father. He was a fervent worker at the local level, registering voters and hauling voters to polling places on Election Day. He was offered offices, but he had no time away from his farm. He discussed the issues of the day with many neighbors and those bringing mares to service. Under Franklin D. Roosevelt, Dad strongly objected to subsidy and never participated in a direct form of subsidy.

Note 3: Dad once told this in church. He was about to sing Riches in the Sky, an old hymn and introduced it this way, "Most of us have gold on earth. I have 4 nuggets: Robert, June, Muriel, Joe." Fast Forward – Joe is retired, Administrator of Kokomo Indiana schools for 28 years, 2 sons and 2 granddaughters. Muriel was a teacher and librarian Logansport, Indiana, 3 children, 2 grandchildren, died in 1993. June was a teacher, farmer and pastor's wife, 5 children, 10 grandchildren. Robert Over-The-Hill and out in the woods in California, wife and 4 nuggets and 12 extenders. Total of 8 degrees.

A Day in the Life of Earl

Earl always crept out of bed by 4:30am. Clad in his winter underwear, farm shoes, bib overalls, shirt and jacket, he stoked the wood stove in the living room, jogged to the barn, lit the lantern, whistled to his dog, stopped to pump a bucket of water and checked to see if anything was frozen. Then he climbed into the haymow and threw great mounds of hay to the waiting horses and cows, carried grain from the grainery and fed and took care of the animals. He checked the cow and calf stanchions. He started the gasoline pump and pump jack, hung the lantern, grabbed his three legged milk stool and squatted under the first of 25 big Holstein cows. After wiping her udder, he would take two to four gallons and squirt eight to ten barn cats with several heavy squirts. They sat upright rarely missing the line of milk. He was relaxed and seemed to store energy while milking. He squeezed the teats in machine gun fashion and accomplished one cow every five minutes. He completed the herd by 7:00am, strained the milk in large 10 gallon steel cans and plopped them into cement tanks ringed by flowing cool water where they remained until 64 degrees was obtained. He then harnessed a team of horses or two, released the cattle out of the milk barn and yelled for me to get the cows to pasture. All of this occurred before the milk truck arrived at 7:45am.

Next, he started the school bus and took it to the house. After a short breakfast and planning with my mother, he ran the bus route, picking up all the kids in rapid fire and unloading them at the warm entry of the big brick school. He then returned to his number two team that he had hitched earlier and went off to work.

He packed a lot of work into the morning and came to the table for lunch at 12 o'clock. His lunch was rarely uninterrupted because he often had calls on the telephone line advising him of a man who had a mare for his stallion at 1 o'clock or another who had a cow in breach birth. Dad always told them he would see them in 5 minutes. These emergencies often found three children and a crying mother waiting with high expectations of Earl Mathias. He returned at 2 o'clock, met the mare for the stallion and followed the others to the field.

Then at 310pm he had to deliver the kids safely back to their homes. Then he met another farmer to service his mare. At 5:30pm the cows were coming down the road to be milked with me following behind the herd. By 7:30pm the cows were released of their burdens of milk He finished a round of chores of some 80-100 animals and fed the imprisoned calves who charged the feeding pails like lions.

He laughed a lot and whistle was his companion. He often turned up his speedometer. He finally blew out the lantern, hurried to the back of the wood shed, grabbed an armful of wood and bundled it into the kitchen where it was stacked for the night. My mom then asked for a large ham hanging from the cellar ceiling. He went down into the night and came up with a large sugar cured ham, cured by Earl Mathias.

After supper he talked on the line for a time, sat down in the wood rocker, grabbed the closest child he could find and hugged, rocked and played until Mom declared bedtime! If she had any sparkle left they went to the piano and practiced some new numbers. It was soon 8:30 or 9pm and sister June was asleep on his lap. Muriel was a baby and pleased with her first night kiss. I was ready for bed.

The Earl of Burton

By 9:00pm mom was in her flannel nightie and the kids were ready to sleep. There were no objections as we climbed or were carried upstairs to a cold kingdom and climbed under 6 inches of covers. After a few good minutes there was no more today.

Earl – Breeder of Belgian Draft Horses

In the late 1920's Earl Mathias bought the first of several registered Belgian Stallions to service the draft mares of the area. By the middle of the 1930's he had at stud the following excellent stallions and in due time the competition became minimal:

Major de Hemel – A 2000 pound stud, well proportioned, highly intelligent, of even temperament, red sorrel in color and destined to sire some 1500 colts in his lifetime. He was a people horse. Everyone liked his friendly nudge and toothful grin. His offspring almost always carried his good temperament traits. His excellence was always ready to be frivolous when a visiting Belgian, Percheron or common mare arrived. He welcomed her heartily with squeals, jumps and grunts. 90% of the conjugals were successful and Major sired some 200 colts per year. In a given farmer's lot and pasture you could see robust and plump little colts frolicking about. If you got up close, there were the remarkable image and manners of Major de Hemel. He was in the greatest demand to stud.

King Albert III – Slightly heavier at 2200 pounds, colored near perfect with flowing white mane and tail against a dark chestnut sorrel body with a blaze face and four white feet. He had a record of numerous championship showings in the show ring and was a close second to Major de Hemel for request of his services. His colts made the strongest show placings. King Albert was imported from Belgium and was named for the king of Belgium. Many farmers wanted colts of his image. However, Major de Hemel remained the favored request, due to his excellent temperament and intelligence.

The Earl of Burton

Benjamin de Houton – A well muscled roan sorrel of near 2000 pounds. This stud had his preferred customers yet was never as popular as his counter parts. He was the picture of a beautiful Belgian with many strong points but in third position.

Jack – For farmers who wished to raise mules Dad kept this large, rangy jack.

During this 10 year period Earl held studs to sire in excess of 3000 colts. This was the period through the Great Depression and just prior to the advent of "the tractor". My father's little brown appointment book supports my memory that every day in spring and summer teams of horses came to our barnyard from several miles around. This was always an exciting time as Dad led the big stallions out, reminded them he was in charge, had the mare teased over a "teasing" pole, and if the mare was in heat the stallion serviced her. No one had to tell me how babies were born. Three weeks later the mare returned to see if she "took" and if so ten months and 1 week later she foaled. After the breeding the visitor's team was watered, harnessed, hitched, and after quite a bit of visitation on crops, horses, weather and oft time humor the visitors left.

Later Dad built a horse trailer some 30 inches high with 4' sides pulled by a series of vehicles, none new nor very respectable. He now widened the territory he could service and soon doubled the number of mares sired. In my mind's eye I remember a rickety trailer and odd vehicle hurrying down country roads with a beautiful stallion, mane flowing, neighing to passing mares. The trailer lurched around curves and corners with the stallion leaning in a manner, never losing his balance and knowing this to be a pleasure trip.

Dad completed his day of milking a large herd of dairy cows, farmed some 300 acres, and annually bred some 400 mares. To understand how all this could happen you would have to have known my father's work habits. It is in vivid recall that I see my father throw the lead rope over Old Major's neck and yell for him to "load up" which he promptly did and usually rode the trailer untied.

The competitions of the horse and colt shows at the County Fair and occasionally the State Fair were the most exciting time for my father and certainly for me. He dressed in new striped bib overalls, new straw hat and sometimes work shoes. He organized the transportation of all the colts, yearlings, and two year olds to be shown from his stallions, making sure all paperwork was properly completed. Following quick chats with dozens of farmers and officials the judges took over. They looked at rows of broad beamed bottoms from the rear and cute faces in front, watching their discipline or lack of same as they were led and turned. They felt their legs, backs and neck, readjusting their order and finally placing the order of finish. Often cheers went up as Major de Hemel and King Albert's foals led the winners. When this happened my father's pride knew no bounds and he smiled for days. I even found him more generous with fair spending money.

In order to exercise the high spirited animals Dad built a large stockade ten feet high and of heavy construction where they were freed from their cages for ½ day at a time. In addition, during the heavy working season we hitched a mare beside one of the stallions in the lead of a five horse hitch for a half day of exercise. This was not always easy and I remember some horrendous horse fights. At least twice runaways instigated by the stallion at the expense of me, a thirteen year old driver. Also my dad would exercise them actively on a long 60 foot lead rope. He ran de Hemel putting him through his antics. This extremely intelligent animal was renowned for his "tricks" and Dad was constantly requested to "show him off". This huge stud would rear up on his hind feet repeatedly at command, walk on his hind feet with front feet and head high in the air, stand in stretched show position, lie down, roll over and at command, shake hands, and count by nodding his head.

Etched upon my memory bank are the rare but real times when one or two stallions broke out of their stalls and charged onto the highway. With my father in hot pursuit and Mom calling the neighbors in the impending direction, my job was to light the lantern, warn traffic to the rear and flag the horses into our lane when Dad returned with them. Conjure, if you will, 2:00 am with two one ton horses charging at full speed down the black road, fighting and biting each other and coming face to face with a sleepy boy driving home from a long date, etc. The worst never happened but several times I choked over near misses before we got them off the road and into reinforced pens.

While traveling in southern Belgium recently (1985) we came into an area where the enormous Belgians were pulling plows, wagons, etc. They appeared to be the grandfather stock of King Albert III, Major de Hemel and Benjamin de Houton. I stopped repeatedly to watch and could imagine my long deceased father also watching with pleasure.

My Cell Multiplication Research – Today, July 2005 this is a subject that will bring discussion in many circles. All have an opinion on the hopes and use of cellular knowledge, the infinite depths of the cellular structure of the human body and the explosive possibilities of regeneration of cells and use of healthy cell replacement to hopefully reoccupy diseased or damaged cells.

Now I am not a scientist, nor widely read and even if I was the outpouring of new studies and scientific findings are so voluminous - volumes are emitted each month that I wouldn't attempt to understand this subject. I simply wish to let you know of my early knowledge of cellular multiplication.

My father subscribed to a horse breeder's magazine and an article caught his attention on experimentation with animal artificial insemination. In the next ten years this practice would sweep the USA. My father felt it would solve his problem by extending the semen of a favored stallion to a mare owner's preference. He registered at a veterinary medical school in Chicago. They were offering a short course, six weeks long for veterinarians and non vets. I must add that my father though not a veterinarian, was a familiar animal consultant. Due to distance, qualified veterinarians were usually not available. In our neighborhood, Dad filled the gap. He performed most functions for large animals, particularly horses and cows. The party line rang day and night for Earl. He harnessed his team and went to help with their cow or horse, their pig or whatever was sick or in difficulty. He was the good neighbor, the Good Samaritan, the cheapest guy out of town.

His absence when he went to school for six weeks was horrendous. But we survived with hired help and neighbors. The day we met the Erie passenger train east at the Rochester depot was very welcome.

The Earl of Burton

He had much to tell us of his stay in Chicago. He told us about the school, what he had learned and his vision for artificial insemination. He brought a gift for each of his children and my mother, Goldie. But, the most imposing item he brought home was a large box three feet high, thirty inches deep and four feet wide. It was polished and lined with velvet and had fasteners to secure items in the interior. In one corner was a fine microscope laying in position next to many stainless steel pieces of veterinary equipment, thermometers, lab supplies, charts and booklets. This was a portable lab, kept under key. It occupied an important corner in our kitchen. Neighbors and family members came by to peek into the strange box Earl had acquired.

Soon my father was fertilizing the eggs of two or more mares with the excess semen from the ejaculation of our stallions. And then the microscope! How it worked was totally unknown to me, and most who came to our house had never seen one before. Dad would use the microscope to check the sperm. By taking a bit of the sperm and putting it between the two glass slides, an amazing picture of the cells emerged, vacillating in and out, overlapping, invading. The cells were reacting, interacting, pulsating, and multiplying. Soon there were more of them. I was a boy of eight when my father showed me these sights in the microscope. I had a new insight into life at its beginning.

In the show ring where the finest colts were promenaded before the lofty judge, my father, the proudest man in town, assisted in arranging the Belgian darlings in rows, all groomed and trained by the owner and Earl, the owner of Major de Hemel and King Albert. Perhaps 20 of Major de Hemel's colts, 20 of King Albert's and 5 of Benjamin's were paraded before the judge, along with perhaps 20 of other competitors. Blue ribbons were most frequently placed around the necks of Major de Hemel's colts. Blues and reds went around the necks of King Albert's colts. The judge based his opinion upon disposition, execution of training, intelligence, vigor, carriage, masculinity or femininity and whatever else makes up a sensational animal. I looked down the line of baby colts and could readily tell those sired by Major and King Albert. Paternal and maternal emphasis is important in bringing to life the best adjusted, the healthiest and most productive.

As a boy I never considered or even thought about these observations for anything other than animals. However, later in life in my role as a school superintendent I often thought how little consideration goes into these equations. It wouldn't be ethical to check for problems of family background microscopically, but it might help if one were to use a little bit of brain power. I've read that 20% of newlyweds don't meet their in-laws until after they wed. That means they know nothing of the health factors, the mental factors, and the religious endowment factor and often are totally careless. A good farmer would never be so inconsiderate of his animal's heritage.

It is totally absurd to calculate that perhaps in 2080 AD one may order a wife who would have all that she is endowed with computerized, and matched with yours and you could, in advance, see your offspring's SAT scores, athletic excellence, musical talent, kindness or belligerence, anger or warmth, work ethic - all on a long check list. No surprises!

In high school Biology I was first introduced to cellular structures, though very primitively. Later, in college Zoology I gathered more information, but superficial.

Today, 2005 under ethical management, not under government idiots such as Hitler, who sought to clone his ideas of a master race, it is hopeful that through man's intelligence we will learn the depths of cellular structure, learning how they can repair and replace.

Earl, One Who Aided Animals

My dad's life was exciting. The landline phone almost always urgently asked for Earl. As soon as I was considered a partner, which was long after I ceased peeing my pants, about age 6 and thereafter I could often weasel my way along to see the sick horse or cow. I would hold the lantern and run errands and I'm sure I often got in the way. But I was all eyes and ears.

There were usually two patients; the family and the sick animal they depended on. They would be crushed if Earl could not fix the animal. It was not uncommon for women and children to crowd around the sad animal and moan. Dad knew the inside of a cow or a horse as well as the outside. He researched both places for the problem. He would check the temperature under the tongue, in the ears or inside the rectum, smell the breath, look in the eyes, push on the stomach and watch it walk a step. He would then prescribe from a bag of home remedies – things that would physic her, things that reduced fevers.

If it was more involved he sent me for a hot water kettle, wash pan and some oil or lard. He promptly stripped his upper limbs and was bare down to the waste. He lathered his arms and shoulders, rinsed, spread oil or grease around his hands and arms, washed the rectum entry and then, greasing his hands entered the opening. He went into the intestines, examined them one to the other, feeling them carefully with his hands. Dad cleared his way, felt carefully, penetrated into the intestinal tracks and cleared all obstructions and complexities. He then gave the family his verdict. Sometimes he could help and sometimes he could not. If the question pertained to the uterus or bladder

The Earl of Burton

and or items of pregnancy he entered likewise by the uterus, felt his way in that strange world where tiny claves or colts originate and are carried to birth, and waste removal, urine and fecal matter are toted off separately. He finally withdrew his arm, washed in soapy lather, dried off and pulled on his shirt in the cold barn. A genuine creator conceived all this and my father understood it a bit.

In the case of problems with the developing fetus, he understood much about the mother and the fetus and after scrubbing could facilitate both. In severe cases he used a block and tackle to pull the fetus. This was usually done in an effort to save the mother cow or horse. Hopefully the fetus would come out alive. His fee was the saved animal or just the opportunity to help a neighbor. He left with a cheery goodnight. We skedewed home and usually went straight to bed. He was soon asleep with a few snores, while I lay in bed replaying the sights and sounds of the day.

For the sake of my interest in old time remedies, I add another memory of that time and place. Dad was called about a horse that had a very sore leg. No vet was available. The horse was a workhorse, owned by a poor family. She had torn her leg on a barbed wire and could no longer stand. The pus and drainage from the swollen leg not only smelled evil but indicated this horse was in deep trouble. Dad took a look, got two block and tackles, two spent plugs and hoisted her off the ground in the driveway of the barn. He got scalding water, lanced her leg and allowed drainage to pursue. He applied a few known remedies for high temperatures and pain. He allowed her to swing until late evening.

Dad then examined her again. He took a hip boot, filled it with fresh cow manure from his daily, cleaned cow barn, salted it and included one or two other (I don't know) properties. He carefully explained the situation and that this was the last chance. They knew the inevitable and gave the go ahead. Dad slipped the boot on, securing it by straps over the neck and the shoulder. Dad added several syringes of water to keep her from dehydrating. Dad said "Folks this is all I have. Call me if needed. I'll look in tomorrow afternoon."

When he returned an excited family said their horse was neighing and calling for something to eat. Dad removed the boot and washed the leg down and a near miracle had transpired. There was little pus, the swelling was down and the horse was feeling much better. Getting a new boot of fresh cow manure, the poultice was reapplied and left for another 24 hours. The horse was then lowered on a pile of hay and washed again. With help he ate. This remedy was known as a last try and had succeeded.

My dad lamented always that he needed something to kill the genus of bacteria. He would be amazed with the ways modern vets can control infections quickly.

Earl, One Who Helped People

Each of the following stories shows the side of my dad that everyone knew best. Whether those in need were family, friends or strangers, he was always there to help.

Double Pneumonia – The winter of 1927 was a hard winter, with lots of snow. To a 6 year old this meant many hours of playing in the snow. On one such day, instead of boarding the bus, the winter wonder world called, with drifts stacked to the fence tops. I called my friends and we ran and jumped in the drifts, then rolled and tunneled and dug out until the bus driver blew his horn. My friends ran and left me, as I could walk home and proceeded to do so, wading in the drifts until the buses passed me by. The next morning I did not feel well. My mother kept me home. Things did not mend and in another day I had fever and was sick. By the next evening I was delirious, had a high fever and was breathing with difficulty. Dr. Loring was called. He drove out, examined me and reported that I was in the early grip of double pneumonia. The good doctor was very serious. I was segregated to a cold room, as many were unsure whether or not pneumonia was contagious. Here I stayed for eight months.

During this time, my mother was pregnant with my sister Muriel. My Aunt Mae, dad's sister came to help as often as she could. But my dad, Earl was my primary caregiver. In addition to looking after the animals, milking the cows and farming the farm, he took care of Robert (me). He fed me. He held me when my mother changed the bed. He bathed me. He put me on the pot. He took me off the pot. And when high fever hallucinations sent fierce animals or large insects or crawling rats into my room, my screams were always answered by my dad. He would come and chase them away with his big arms, caressing words and just his presence made it all seem better. In very bad times he slept with me, holding me tight. He often hummed church tunes. I then slept. The horribly long and lonely days and nights crawled across the calendar. Finally, in April, Dr. Loring told me, "Son, you have fought a tough fight and I think you are going to make it. We'll know for sure over the next 1 ½ months". I continued to improve and when the warmth of summer came I was again chasing after my father.

Jim Nichols - One morning at breakfast a call came in for dad and the sheriff said "Earl, I have a man that just today was released from prison and he is here and his wife and two sons are here and they have no place to go and almost no possessions. Do you think you have anything to give these people cover?"

This slowed dad. He said he knew nothing. He ask why this fellow was in prison and the sheriff responded "He put a man in the hospital for living with his daughter for over a year, getting her pregnant and then deserting her". Dad said, "Ory, I have nothing". Then he remembered an old house down the road where the rats and the squirrels lived. The doors are off; windows are out the rain helps itself. It has a 3-holer in the back, I think. Water well is good but the pump is bad.

What will they do to eat? Ory was vague – "Well Earl they are desperate. I'll bring them out if you'll permit". He did and they were horrified at this house but willing to clean if a few things could happen. Dad went home, called the party line minister and a few church people. He told them about this. They indicated the Nichols could move into the church basement until Sunday – this was Tuesday. We'll try to get a stove in the house and close it up somewhat. You must scrub it completely and get help to do it. For 4 days some church men and women and the Nichols and dad fetched some fixings and the doors were made to close, a few of the windows were glassed and the rest were boarded up. The chimney was made useful and the walls were scrubbed but still porous. An old stove was put in, donated by the Hudkins. Besides those things, they brought a grub steak from their gardens and cellars. Enough to keep them alive for 2-3 weeks. They loaded everything into Dad's school bus and he jitneyed it to the old house.

They remained over 3 years, made due worked for any one needing a farmhand. Mrs. helped mom some. They had a garden and when he got a job in another town they vacated the house for one much better. Much later I heard they were making it and the boys were entering high school. They were Catholics and had a little shrine in the corner of their living room with a picture of the Virgin Mary and Christ and a votive candle sometimes. Jim was red headed and hot headed and almost destroyed the man who wronged his daughter. They came in 1931 and left in 1934.

The Escape from a Fiery Home – One night about 11pm dad was returning in his school bus from one of our neighbor's, where he had been assisting a mare that was having a slow fold. Just east of the church he noticed light in the black sky. He turned in that direction and soon recognized flames. It was the Cook home. He hurried up their lane. As he hurried into the yard, Mr. Cook came out telling him his wife was in the house in a very, very sick condition. He showed dad where she was. Dad threw a wet blanket over his head and rushed into the flaming house. He pulled the bed across the room to the exit door, grabbed the sick woman and took her out the door. He took her across the road and put her in his school bus. He drove her and her two boys to a neighbor's house. When he returned the house was consumed. Mrs. Cook lingered for months. Then she died. Dad's arms and hands were burned, making it very difficult for him to milk for several days. Mom and I helped out. Each of us would milk 3-4 cows, while he milked the other dozen.

Grandpa Earl

The Earl of Burton

Earl During the World Wars

World War I - In 1916 the USA joined the British, French and allies and slowly marshaled a fighting force. By 1917 they had units facing the experienced armies of the Germans etc. Accompanying our efforts was a wicked flu that spread throughout the United States populace and military. The death toll from the flu was greater than from the war battles.

By 1918 we had well trained troops and leadership on the fronts and bolstered by our friends, we brought the Germans to their knees in Paris. Just 60 days earlier Earl Mathias was a recruit, going to help. He was 24 years old and already an incredible farmer, farming with his father. However, he felt the army needed him and believed the fierce Germans that threatened the armies had to be stopped. He was sent to William Henry Harrison Camp near Indianapolis for training. He was scheduled to take a trip to Europe, but with the armistice in 1918 they stopped further shipping of troops and supplies. By November he had been discharged and sent home to Burton.

For years his kids sometimes looked in an old dresser drawer and saw an old uniform with an old pin on the front and a military hat.

World War II - Upon my graduation from high school, my family and my girl Lois sat proudly. My dad had enjoyed and applauded my athletics, was pleased with my good grades and had reached a milestone through my graduation.

His remodeled house had running water, an inside toilet and bathroom, an extended kitchen with a modern washing machine, a freezer and cabinets in the kitchen. There were grand porches on all entries, each painted and trimmed. There was a new car in the driveway.

The barn had been improved. It boasted a new big silo, new milk cooler, a small electric feed grinder and most of its doors had recently been painted red. It was quite an addition and was accompanied by his first new tractor and a lot of equipment. Most horses were now phased out, hog facilities were enlarged and he no longer drove the school bus. He now owned several parcels that he had once rented. The knowledge and professional help had facilitated insect control and yields had catapulted by the application of fertilizers.

Dad kept a tight rein on his checkbook and now kept money safely secured in the new bank. He was a welcome farmer figure in this bank. The officers had his name on a list of solid investors. He had restored some $700 he had lost when the old bank closed its doors. His savings was now on top of $850 restoration by directors of the bank. He set a standard and could borrow to meet his feed and fertilizer needs. After the sale of a truck load of fat hogs Earl would stop by the bank and deposit $422, the full proceeds. He walked through the revolving doors, removed his old hat, brushed his seven hairs across his bald spot, brushed the pig straw off his pants and hoped the pig manure wouldn't expose him. Then he ran into the Double Dip, got a big ice cream cone, crawled in his truck and hurried home to milk.

At 48, he leaned back and observed his success. Then he turned on his first radio and heard an electrifying announcement that brought forth "The Japs have attacked Pearl Harbor". The talk of Japanese invasion spread faster

The Earl of Burton

than Morse code to every part of the USA and within 24 hours an unusual phenomenon occurred. Hundreds of thousands of farm boys, city boys, town boys, students, employed and unemployed, responded and the enlisting centers were flooded. Baer Field, a military base at Fort Wayne, Indiana was nearby and ½ million arrived requesting enlistment. One of them was me, James Robert Mathias (JRM), who with Lois by my side ask for immediate enlistment and to train as a pilot. Many were deferred and JRM was told to finish college and they would call when an opening and training could occur. I was called to serve in 1943.

This revolutionized America and we were soon a leader in World War II. Several efforts were made for more materials and on several fighting fronts all over the globe our military arrived with the best equipped planes, submarines and ships. Men and woman power were essential. There were few seekers of work now. Mothers and sisters left the kitchen for the war jobs.

Dad took his old hat off, looked around, scratched his head and pondered "I've got to support Robert and the army. The farm has to feed the soldiers and the workers". He put his old hat back on, climbed on his tractor and vowed to see her through. He put on the nightlights and ran the tractor until midnight. Two sisters were in college and my brother was now a basketball player at Rochester High School.

During the depression he had several times joined the cheese gang at Armour & Company. They called him now and ask if he could help them turn out a large order for the armed forces. He finished milking at 715pm, ate a bit, climbed into his car and seven miles later entered Armour's large creamery. Shortly, in waist high waders and white apparel he entered the whey tub. It was very large, perhaps 80X40. He manned a currying cheese rake for hours, then drained them into bats and dried a bit and wrapped them before drying. Two more whey tanks were emptied and finally two box cars were loaded with boxes of cheese. He imagined that cheese was going to me and Glen and all the other boys of Burton and Rochester.

He returned to his farm to milk at 430a with an optimum feeling. After a few hours of sleep he went back to the Armour Cheese factory. He did that for three days.

Earl's Dog, Bill
May, 1938

Bill was 3 years old and already had a reputation for being a highly intelligent and disciplined dog. He minded my father as near as he could determine his will, and worked whenever Dad called. He helped Dad get cows in and out of the cow barn. He would take the cows 1/4 mile to the overnight pasture down the road. When Dad got up (usually 4:30AM) Bill would hustle down the road and in 30 minutes he had rounded up the cows, driven them down the road and into our lane. Many passers-by marveled at this herd of cows and the big black and white dog that was in charge.

One day, a shotgun shot rang out pretty close and I heard the yell of a dog. I ran from the grainery, where I was cleaning out the grain bins, making way for the new grain that we'd harvest in a few days. Shortly, Bill came limping into the lane and as he passed me I could see his shoulder was bleeding. He refused to let me examine him. He went to the horse tank where he drank lushly and then went into the barn and licked his shoulder. It was almost certain Frank Rerick had shot him for hunting rabbits on his property. He had often made threats to this end at the store. No one thought he would shoot E. Mathias' dog unless he was drunk. Dad was unhappy, but not willing to take action against Frank. Bill's shoulder healed with Dad's doctoring and in 3 weeks he was as good as ever.

The summer rolled into August and I was on the threshing ring. Mom and the kids had gone to the church to practice for Children's Day. Oren Richard, a neighbor was passing by and saw Frank Rerick in our lane. As he watched, Bill

43

ran and grabbed Frank's leg, as Frank was threatening Bill with a club and rocks. Oren yelled at Bill, who stood back. Oren came to see about Frank who was hobbling toward the road, screaming loudly. Frank reeked of liquor.

Frank did not stop to get a pint of milk for several days and he failed to show up at the store each evening where he was a regular B.S.er. The threshing was now at Uncle Wills. A neighbor tried to locate Frank to help him scoop grain. Frank didn't answer when he honked his horn at his house. I told Dad all of this and he went to Frank's, where he found him in a filthy bed quite sick with high fever, a torn calf muscle and infection forming. Frank was in bad shape, mostly out of his head, swearing incoherently. Dad hurried home and called Aunt Mae. They took Frank to Dr. Stinson (6 miles away). Mom called Floyd Reese to help me milk.

They returned from Dr. Stinson's about 9:00PM. Mom and Aunt Mae had gone in and put clean sheets on Frank's bed. Dad stayed with him, giving him medicine during the night and the next day. Dad and I tried to feed him, but he wanted nothing. He was very sick the next night, so Dad and I took him to town and Dr. Stinson put him in an overnight care room. The following morning about 11:00, the office called and told my mother that Frank had died. She came to Willie Kennels' place, where we were thrashing. Dad went to town to see the coroner and take Frank to the undertaker, Val Zimmerman.

I helped Dad take Bill to the vet to have him examined for rabies. First we put him in the back seat of our Plymouth, but Bill snarled and did not like the odor where Frank had been, so we put him in the front between us. Dad was concerned about the liability, etc. The Sheriff-Coroner discussed the issue with Oren Richard, the witness. Oren

The Earl of Burton

knew my Dad, Frank and even Bill. The coroner did not charge my Dad and felt the dog was doing his duty. Frank's reputation as a drunk was not good and he was in bad health. It was determined that his death was from heart complications induced perhaps by an infection in his leg.

For some time we thought they might put Bill away, but this great dog remained in charge of our farm for many years and as far as I know never bit anyone again.

Note: Frank Rerick was a bachelor who lived by hunting and renting his ground out. He lived with his blind mother until she died and thereafter probably took few baths and seldom washed his clothes. He was a good story teller, although he lied a lot and caused me a lot of grief by telling tales about me that were not true. Most of the time, I didn't like him any better than Bill did. One time he poured pure turpentine on my pony's tail after he had rubbed it raw with a corncob and she ran like she was crazy! My mother said we should pray for Frank after he died but I had a hard time, although I tried.

Bill was a strong-bodied white dog with black and brown patches and a strong head. I've had several good dogs, but Dad's was the smartest in the whole world, I think. He only ate what Dad gave him - a drink of fresh cow's milk and a hand of cracklings and whatever he could catch hunting.

One time Bill went with me to run my traps in our ditch on a very cold morning. I fell through thin ice over a tile ditch entry where I had a mink trap set. Due to the muck I had trouble getting out. Bill barked and barked and left me. I broke the ice and waded up the ditch to a shallow place where I climbed out, but not before I was wet to my armpits. As I was coming to the house, about frozen to death, I met Dad (who yelled at me) along with Bill. That was the only time Dad ever went looking for me, but Dad said Bill told him I needed help!

Another time, Dad was loading a big stock truck with fat hogs at our place. Near the end, Bill was putting pressure on them and ran up the chute and into the truck. After he drove the last hog into the truck, Lee tripped the gate. No one noticed as it was night and Bill rode with the hogs to Rochester and Ike Duffey's Yards, where everyone was really surprised to see Bill pop out when the gate opened.

CHAPTER 2

It Was the Worst of Times

The Great Depression 49

The Winter Wood 55

The Blizzard of 1926 62

The Rains Came 69

The Milk Strike 73

The Great Depression

Today we struggle to learn a trade or means of making a living for our families and ourselves. Young people struggle to learn where they fit in, how they will be educated and whom they will socialize with. The old people retire and go on to enjoy the Golden Age. Life has not always been so simple.

In fact, life was an awesome struggle when in January 1929 the economy of our nation was very near collapse. The stock market folded, destroying support of the dollar. The picture was somewhat this:

- 80% of the USA factories closed
- Unemployment was up to 50,000,000 persons, or one out of three
- All were without any benefits – no working man's compensation, no health insurance, no welfare
- Banks were locked and most closed
- Money circulation was reduced by 50% as well as the supply of funds
- Commerce ground to a crawl
- The streets and highways had very little traffic
- Desperate people walked, biked or hitchhiked – seeking places for work or traveling home to their origins and relatives
- The only increases were in suicides, bread lines and disenfranchised people.
- Nature joined the attack - one of the worst droughts in our history occurred during this time and lasted 3 years or more in some areas. Corn never reached knee high. Cattle and other livestock and people died. Insects- grasshoppers, locusts, ants, cicadas

- etc. launched serious attacks, destroying all vegetation in some areas. Enormous winter blizzards and summer hail bombarded the nation
- Farmers lost their farms by the thousands. They could not meet their mortgage payments.

What hath God wrought? Or Man?

During this time I was a boy on a farm near a railroad in Indiana. The trains continued to run, but in less numbers. They weren't carrying coal, foodstuffs, or retail merchandise to stock stores, but dragged flat cars full of men, fathers, brothers and a few women. They went from area to area seeking a job to support the near starving family back home. We watched thousands of passersby on the flatcars or boxcars as the rails sailed by. The only food they could bring on the train was jerky, tobacco and bags of root vegetables. There were few drunks as no intoxicants were available and they were unable to carry a bottle while running and grappling onto a moving train. It was hazardous for all, especially for the old, the weak and sick, the intoxicated and the uncoordinated. It took some athletic ability to "Catch a Freight". It was not a pleasant means of travel and was extremely dangerous and difficult, especially for women and children few of which joined the throng of rail traffic. We once saw a man who had a 10-year-old girl with him. We saw perhaps a dozen hardy women go by. The services, of course, were nil – no bathroom on the train, no seats, no beds, no conductor to keep you oriented, no steps or help to board, no dining car. There were railroad police, called Bulls, whose job it was to evict non-paying passengers, keep them from coming aboard and be on the lookout for criminals! The Bulls were greatly outnumbered.

The Earl of Burton

Our train siding had a waterspout where the steam engines took on water. This was near Loyal, a town that had an elevator, a general store, a depot, perhaps a dozen houses, a railroad with 3 tracks – 2 main lines and 1 as siding for loading and dropping cars. We had a "Jungle", called so as a gathering place for the hobos near the railroad siding. The train slowed there and they could jump off or on and rest, sleep, hopefully eat, sometimes hide and sometimes die.

My parents forbade me to enter the "Jungle" on pain of a hard spanking with Dad's razor strap. Yet my chums and I went one day to the willow tree edge, peeked in and a few "Bos" were there. We saw this was not a first rate hotel, but a jungle of dirty men, a collection of trash with logs to sit on. There were piles of rotted cardboard, a few boards and brush from hereabout bushes, all used to make lean-tos. Nearby was a smoldering fire. These offered the most protection from rain, snow, ice and sleet. There were old tarps, covers, blankets, hay, etc. and they burrowed in like animals during the Indiana subzero winter weather, sometimes not surviving until morning.

Two of the men we saw were smoking – what, I think, was a local wild seeded plant that was almost impossible to keep lit and smelled horrible. This plant was common to our area and many of us boys had experimented with it! Another of the men was trying to pull a tooth from a buddy with a piece of wire, as he was suffering. As I watched, a "bo" said to me, "Hey Boy, you got a chunky ass – maybe I will cut a steak out of it!" We left pronto! And watched from afar afterward.

Almost a year later, Zeke and I got brave and took another careful look into the "Jungle" on a Sunday afternoon. There were a bunch of guys home in the "Jungle" and one of them was talking to the group. I guess he was a preacher or maybe just a troubled man trying to ease the pain. He was rallying their spirits by telling them of the Lord above and promising that He could give them comfort. I don't remember much, but he had their attention and many prayed aloud and in earnest. I felt very sorry for them. We crept away!

Food at our "Jungle" was begged by a line of men who constantly arrived at our back door. They ask for anything to eat. Often they were close to starving after being on the rails for 2-3 days or more. Most of the food beggars first asked for work, then food. They were working men who were desperate for food. Sometimes Dad took on a Bum for a day or two, but this was a challenge as many did not know of farm duties and had to be supervised. However, a man who hailed from Georgia had once farmed, so Dad kept him for 2 weeks. He slept in the grainery. He was an able and willing worker, skilled with horses and other farm duties and Dad often said he wished he could have several such workers. However, he couldn't afford to stay long, for all we could do was give a bit of food and that didn't help his family back home. My mother was bombarded by these backdoor beggars and was fearful of them. There was hardly enough to keep her family going, but she would give whatever she could spare - a few slices of bread and black strap molasses in a dipper for spread and sometimes apples or potatoes.

Some of the people of the "Jungle" and boxcar travelers were angry men, almost animals, desperadoes, who were on the fringe of life and robbed or killed at will. The local sheriff sometimes visited the "Jungle" and often was on the lookout and even posted pictures at the General Store for the desperadoes. However, most of these beggars, only a year or two ago had been good workers or farmers or businessmen or executives. They ran the factories and businesses of America. They were good, intelligent fathers of families. Now they were desperate, striving to get a job. Americans then as well as today were charitable, BUT almost none had anything to give. Farmers, I believe, in our neighborhood gave all or more than they could - excess grain, garden crops, wood, etc. They understood that they were not far from wearing the same hat and every year some of them were swept into the drowning river of unemployment. Horrible days happened in our community when a sale bill announced a Farm Sale. This happened with a farmer couldn't pay his mortgage and debts. The farm and all its belongings were sold to cover the debt. This happened to 2 of our close neighbors. It was a sad time. No locals bid, only dealers.

Dad was a dairy farmer and milked by hand 25-30 cows and sent the milk to the city. During these times the market was almost nil. He always mixed some in the hog slop and always had a 3-gallon can for visitors, with a cup hanging beside. He also put out a pail of cracklings each week. Visitors relished this, needless to say, and our place had a reputation as a favorite stopping place. He must have given a thousand gallons of milk over 8 years. He also had grits for the dogs, which were remains of the butchering where he made crisp cracklings.

Dad was a committed Christian and had a Big Heart! He treated these people as brothers and never flinched. If a horse died, he butchered it and gave it to the "bos". He was a non-professional veterinarian and often cared for their bad sores, injuries and infections. My mom and dad enabled them to write to their families by keeping paper, pencils and envelopes in the grainery door. We would stamp them and give them to the rural mailman. I believe we sent a lot of their letters as Mom said her egg money went for "Bos" stamps. Once the mailman left an envelope with 100 stamps for the "Bos".

In the big cities the suffering was worse. We had cellars and gardens and animals; they had no means of getting food from the ground. In our neighborhood, the mailman still came, the huckster wagon still came, our preacher still preached and I still went swimming in the creek daily. The world continued to spiral, but it now wobbled!!

The Winter Wood

A snow covered freight train slowed and crawled into the siding and shortly a passenger train to Chicago streaked past. And as it did two bundles of snow lopped off the freight into a ditch drift and all was briefly quiet. Then the piles of snow up heaved and struggled down to a fence emerging itself some two feet above the snow. Then the appurtenances moved down the fence and lunged through the snow.

The housedog, a terrier sounded an alert and a lady long widowed hurried to see "What on earth?" She put on her blue bonnet and heavy shawl and with a "Hello" she unlocked the back porch door, picked up a broom and confronted the snow bums. They pleaded for food and agreed they would work for the same. Mae next started sweeping them off, removing a few bundles and then examined their real looks – a grubby pair, one surrounded in an old dirty bear skin coat. She heard and saw half frozen beards, faces and feet as she brought them onto her back porch. As they perceived food and relief from present agonies were possible, they were polite, having only one motive – food. Mae left them outside until she had prepared the food. Then and only then, did she unlock the back door and welcome them into her kitchen and the smell of food. Leading off with gopher bread one dropped to his knees and prayerfully called Mother of Heaven Mary, Thank You. He then went to the food - a watery bit of soup, coffee and a pot of cracklings. They ate and ate until there was no more. While they were eating Mae had rung up Tom Spurlock at his store just across the tracks and reported to him of her new guests. Tom acted as the sheriff of X

Germany Station, now called Loyal and kept an eye on strange drifters. He told Mae to take care and keep in touch.

As it was late afternoon and the day was receding. She rang Tom again and said, "What should I do with them? They want to work to get food and rest". Tom said "Give them cover for the night and lock them away from you". She quickly did so by getting out the cowhide and an old blanket, throwing them on empty springs on the back porch. There was not a complaint from the "bos". By six o'clock, after more watery soup, bread and coffee they passed out in the coldest bed in Loyal. But soon the body warmth of two bodies between animal skins and the old blanket kept the hunger down and never a word until sun hit the bungalow at dawn.

The phone jingled and Tom said "Earl Mathias could use those "bos" for 2-3 days to get in wood. He will feed them and sleep them in the barn". Mae relayed and the "bos" were willing. At about 930am Vern Castleman was passing in his sleigh boat and allowed for the two riders to get aboard. He agreed to take them to his brother Earl's farm. Vern pointed to the great unpainted buildings with a barn lot in the rear and they started off without tracks to follow, arriving at the lane where Big Bill, dad's dog called a stop. Dad said Ok and the two strong creatures appeared for Dad's inspection. Dad shook hands and welcomed the pair. He was friendly and inquired of any skills they might have like cutting wood with a cross cut saw or axe. The talk in 10 degree weather was brief and he led them to his big mud boat. He told them to sit on the floor. He and I stood and I clung to his sturdy leg. He yelled at Bob and Betty, a big tough team. They struggled through the snow to the woods where dad dropped the gate and the team drove non-stop through the woods. Far back in the drifts and whitened

The Earl of Burton

trees, dad's team caught snow loaded branches that dropped bushels of snow down our necks. Dad yelled and laughed and said this was fun, but the "bos" never grinned. Dad called a halt beside a very large tree of some 4-foot girth at the base sprawled face down in the snowy earth. First he ask all to tramp around the fallen giant. The "bos" brushed snow and stomped. Dad and I finally got close enough to use a cross cut saw across the butt of the great log, standing in snow up to our arm pits. We got the saw moving, cut deep although I was quite short for the job and had trouble connecting on that saw for long and after 45 minutes dad called for a replacement, taking a "bo" in my place. Now the "bo" Norv was 5'10' and maybe with a few days of milk and food he would scale 160 pounds. Although he didn't understand the first effort, he soon followed dad's instructions and off went the large blocks one by one. I heard Dad tell the "bo" that he was doing good, but when he wore out I took two more short turns. By the time the dinner bell sounded at 12 o'clock we had cut a couple of short blocks. Dad turned Bob and Betty toward the barn and they were most willing as it was still about 15 degrees above zero and standing in such weather is not enjoyable, even for horses.

My mother had dinner ready but about the "bos" she had doubts. She left them at the back door. She never let them get near her children. She trusted none of them, certainly never at first, only after they had proven themselves. We had no back porch so they had to enter her kitchen to eat. She had a place at the wash pump where she had two chairs and there they ate gladly. What did they eat? Milk was abundant. The food was usually sauerkraut and a big pot of soup beans and bread. For the bread she included homemade apple butter and after the hungries were satisfied, dad's blessing on the table was appreciated by all.

By mid-afternoon we went home with a load and made our way to the woodhouse heaving a number of blocks and dad had the "bos" take the ax and split the wood into fine wood for the kitchen stove. They put it in the front corner of the wood house, leveling the wood and destroying Bill's bed.

Then dad and all took Bob and Betty back to the woods. Dad kept the saw flying with Norv. I was sawed out and laid under the old rug in the mud boat. Norv could not go as long as dad but between them they finished and I didn't have to go back. Peter, the other "bo" was an ax man. He trimmed and split and cut small pieces. Dad was satisfied but only glad when we loaded a big load and headed in. I was disappointed when we got there to not find a warm seat before the stove. Instead, my dad went straight to new tasks. We emptied the wood, unharnessed the horses, unhitched the team and then feeding commenced. It began with a pleading niggardly by the horses for their grain and continued until I dropped 3 large corn ears into their box and a big scoop of oats to each. I liked this job, although carrying a bushel was almost to much for me. Dad said we had to make more trips, but he never did and I didn't intend to either. The animals were unified, all hay dropped and distributed. Silage was dropped and Norv said he'd throw it down, but he had never seen it done before and didn't know what to do. Pete went to see but he couldn't figure out how to climb up the silo, so I fearfully climbed up the icy steps on the outside of the silo. The silage was frozen so solid that Norv couldn't get it loose. Norv and I worked together to dig it out and started throwing down the silage, causing it to rain huge piles of silage. There was no danger, but "bos" Pete started yelling. He was under the rain of silage. Dad then milked 26 cows and I milked 2

The Earl of Burton

Dad showed the "bos" their bed in the cow barn. It was on a four-foot bench used for buckets and corn. Warmed by the bodies of 30 big Holsteins the temperature was kept above freezing, maybe 35 degrees. Pete and Norv felt they had attained a real for sure home.

The next morning dad disturbed them at 430am when he got up to milk and feed. He enlisted them to help clean and water all and shortly he queried them to see if they would like to go to church. The preacher would ride in at 10 o'clock and anyone who could get this way was welcome. My mother and the girls preferred to study at home but dad combed his hair, washed up, hitched up and welcomed the "bos". He and I set sail in a whirl of snow to the church where we found three mud boats and horses tied to the fence. The minister had a small fire in the basement and gave his sermon to some 14 brave souls including the "bos". The piano player was not present and dad led the hymns a capello in a strong alto voice. He filled the room and beyond with music.

Anxious to get home to our cozy fire and family the horses went at a lop and soon Bob and Betty were tied in their stalls. Dad had playtime with little sister and me a spell by the fire with mom. The bus rested in the warm cow barn.

Sun up Monday and dad introduced the "bos" to splitting wood for the kitchen stove. It was slow going at first, but Pete led the way and by mid morning both guys were splitting dry wood in large amounts. Mom was pleased when she saw the pile corded for her stove.

It remained cold with the thermometer climbing to 32 degrees by 4pm Monday. Then it dipped down a little bit overnight, then warmed up more the next day. Some men came in and plowed the roads Wednesday and we were unlocked. The milkman came and loaded two days of milk. Dad started the model T ford and drove the "bos" to uncle Lloyds around the corner. He bid the "bos" adieu, thanking them vigorously. He loaded them with milk, sorghum molasses and bread. They waited at Mae Knight's back porch. The next morning a belching freight slipped into the siding to make room for the 10 o'clock limited to Chicago and the two bos slipped onto the freight as the fast train whizzed by.

I was glad by Monday that I didn't have to split that kitchen wood. Thanks Pete and Norv.

The Earl of Burton

Bob and Betty Look Alikes

The Blizzard of 1926

I was awakened in the boisterous night. I heard the wind caroling past my window howling like 40 wolves on a hot chase. I jammed down in my heavy covers, forming a fetal position in the pit of my straw tick. It was cold. I heard my father downstairs stoking the fire, plopping another large old chunk into the already feisty fire. To survive I kept wrapped with covers and was 103% inundated.

Again, I awoke, this time to daylight. I unearthed one eye. I was encouraged. I heard mom call, "Robert, come". I checked out of my tick, brushed off a skiff of snow that had drifted from a cracked window and hurried downstairs to the rosy, red stove. Quickly I dove into my overalls and wool shirt. Then my mother said "Come, look what is outside!" With one sock on and one in hand I ran to see. Half of the pane was snow covered, but the other opened to a miracle. A new world had been born last night. It was a white, white world. The yard, the fields, the trees, the telephone pole, the barn roof - all heavenly white. The only non-white was the wind swept corner of our barn, which was unpainted and now etched in white.

My mother saw my crossed legs and said "Robert, do you have to go to the toilet?" I said yes and she said "I do too". She opened the door that led the way to the outhouse. She shut it quickly as the snow and cold rushed in. In that brief glance she could not see the outhouse or the path that led to it. There were only hills and cliffs of snow. She got a metal pee pot from the closet, 3 gallons and this satisfied our needs for this morning.

The Earl of Burton

A while later my dad struggled to the back door, scooped away the snow, blew his nose loudly, brushed a pile of snow off his coat, kicked off his overshoes and came in. "This is a blizzard!" he said. "It must be 10 degrees below zero and it is still blowing. I fed the cows and horses and milked, but I couldn't get to the three sows in the hog house by the wood. There are huge banks of snow over the hog house, maybe 12 feet high." He went on, "There can't be school. The roads and lanes are not passable. Mother, do you have water in the kitchen stove? If I have to pump it I may get a bucket full but it will freeze very quickly. Use only what you must." This was a severe time. A monumental sky full of snow had been dumped over northern Indiana. A horrendous cold front from the Artic had come over the great lakes, blasting the people of Indiana, Michigan, Wisconsin and Ohio. Years later it was historied as the worst in a half century.

At our house all was well for the moment. Some 100 animals or more were close to feed. Water was within 18 feet down below them in a well, sheltered with protection but certainly not insulated. Responsibility for the safety of all was a young man and woman who knew they had to try to get through the rigors of this blizzard. They were oblivious of the real challenge. For they didn't yet know that there was no radio, no telephone, no communication with neighbors, towns or cities, no mail and no other resources. In addition to our survival, the young man, my father also had responsibility for his mother a ½ mile away. Beyond that he worried about his brothers and sisters, close friends and the helpers who worked for him often.

My youthful concern was something else. From the inside, I window shopped, marveling at this new and bright world with no birds, no people or animals. No telephone lines were visible. Only snow wrapped 3 inches deep and every so often a pile of snow 5 feet deep airborne. Below our house was the grazing place for the colts and cows. Now that pasture was frequented by little tussocks maybe a foot high, with snow concentrated 3-4 feet above the fields and we thought they were Eskimo igloos. Our woods which backed up to this particular pasture had large hardwood trees of oak, birch, elm and others, each now arrayed in their new costumes. In early fall my mother had taken my sister June and I for a stroll through a panoply of beautiful colors in this wood. Then in November I thought they had died as their leaves had fallen and they were stark naked. Now in January miraculously they had new clothes, all gleaming white. The trash and limbs were secreted by snow. It was a place fit for a snow man and I could envision elves playing and running in style.

By 10 o'clock little of the landscape had changed and I had a persuasion to see the outdoors first hand. At 5 years of age I had already attacked snow drifts. But my mom denied as it was still below zero. Dad had a path to the barn and spent most of the morning there. He looked after all his animals and found them all to be ok except one yearling colt. The colt had braved the storm, ran into some implements that were covered with snow, broken his leg and died. Two calves were born in the barn at 20 below zero. The haymow, silo and inside corn cribs were full. No milkman could pick up our fifty to sixty gallons of milk daily. The cans of milk froze. Dad then poured the milk chunks in a trough for the pigs.

Once Dad was insured of our well being, his thoughts turned to his mother. He told mom that he had to get over to her place. He harnessed his biggest team, using the strongest horses. He uncovered the stone boat from the

The Earl of Burton

snow. He hitched the team to the snow boat and worked it out of the barnyard and into the pasture. He had to go through the pasture as the lane was at least four feet deep in snow. They entered through an opening in the barbed wire fence. He then forced the team to go through 2 ½ –3 feet of snow until he reached the road about ¼ mile away. The road was raised at this point and had less snow. Here he had to cut the fence again, a very difficult task. He got the team through the fence and onto the road. It was far below zero as he struck out toward his mother's house to give help.

From my sight he and his two big Belgians were out to fight the worst storm ever. I yearned to be with him. He later related a rugged trip. There was a drift where the horses couldn't emerge and one horse fell and couldn't get up. He unhitched them and whipped them severely with his lines, causing them to thrash and get to their feet. He then pulled them out backwards. He tied them when he could go no further and struggled on foot through the snow to his mother's house. She admitted a weary man encased in snow and ice. She soon recognized her son, Earl. She needed medicine which seemed hopeless as the nearest pharmacy was 6 miles away. She shared that a neighbor ½ mile away used the same medicine. Dad saddled Grandma's buggy horse Heidi and rode her through the snow drifts to the neighbors. He was able to get a small amount of medicine and in the midst of a renewed storm he struggled back to his mother's. It was nearing 4 o'clock when he left the saddle horse behind. Again, on foot he struggled back to his team then drove them furiously through a blinding storm back to our road. From there he continued to Uncle Lloyd's house. He left his team there and borrowed a saddle horse. He rode the horse back through the cut fence, across the pasture and to our barn. He was always capable and this was no exception. After a bit of food and thawing, he milked some 25 cows, bedded the animals and returned for supper, dreary, but alert at 8 pm. This night was the worst of all times and Dad's perilous journey was soon erased as the snow drifted higher and broader. But his problems were not over. Both wells had now frozen. The cows and horses could exist on snow, but the house water supply was dwindling. Mom needed wood for the fire, so she could melt snow for water. The wood in the wood house was encased in snow and frozen hard and she could not get it loose. The big chunks that held fire were gone and we were in serious need of wood. Dad took a big sledge hammer and knocked the blocks of wood loose and carried them into the kitchen. The house water was replenished with melted snow and she kept the water oven at least part full in this way. Her baby lay in a basket by the kitchen stove, unaware of the blizzard outside. Food was plentiful as the cellar was full of cured hams, carrots, potatoes and other foods, all continuously supplemented by our beautiful milk supply.

The third night came and it was severe. We hunkered down, fired the stove, keeping it red all the time, slept in the living room and heard the manacles of the storm clash and bite all night. We were awakened by Dad at 6 o'clock. He was going out to see if he could get to the barn. He did and returned to report that the wind had died down. By Monday it was above zero and the sun was trying to come out. Dad was lighthearted. It was 15 degrees above zero and there was full sun. He hitched his team to the snow boat and cracking his whip above his horse's heads, followed his earlier route to his mother's. He checked on his mother, sisters and others in the area. Some were good, some not so good.

The Earl of Burton

By the next morning it was assured that the blizzard had exhausted itself. The sun made it possible for mom and me to emerge. Dad built a fire around the well, thawing the pipes and by the next day we had water in 32 degree weather. Several snow boats and sleighs could be seen passing by. Within a few days we knew the crisis was ending as early trucks ventured out of the towns. There were no deaths in our community during the storm. However, Grandma died 3 weeks later.

And now a story for "Outhouse Storm History". A week after the blizzard Mom and I tried to find the path to our outhouse. T'was a pleasure romping in the snow. We took turns pushing the snow all the way out to the cherry trees, then along the rickety fence to the outhouse. We couldn't see the outhouse even when we reached it. We began to dig. Mom decided someone had left the door open. Sure enough after more scooping we found the door. Now all we had to do was get the snow out of the outhouse. Finally we got most of it abolished and could close the door. We even located a part of the old Sears Roebuck catalog, although unreadable. This dreary effort brought forth the revered edifice that we all hurried to by day or night, snow, sun or rain. It was a 2-holer somewhat private, but cold and windy. For me, the worst part of the blizzard was that we could not get to our outhouse and had to use the chamber pot. I have to admit that I hated like sin to get out of my straw tick and sit on an ice cold pot! After 70 years of this earlier system I cast a vote for modernity. The snow bank over this fixture remained for one month.

For me, a boy of 5 this storm brought the most beautiful day in January I ever remembered. We created 8 or 9 animals on the afternoon we cleared the path to the outhouse. We played a game looking for snow shaped images and I found 4 and my mother found 4. My images were an elephant, a polar bear, a great big thing and maybe a dead cow. My mother saw a snowbird, a pig, an umbrella and she couldn't decide the last one.

On a bigger basis I don't know much. Many people died, many animals died and those in the city suffered terribly. Our preacher said the storm told us that one must always be prepared. I agreed but I heard there were maybe 500,000 cows that died of cold and starvation when farmers with herds out on the range could not get feed to them. How could they prepare? T'was a deal, unh? Glad we had a good Dad to see us through.

The Rains Came

In 1926, my father was a hard-working Indiana farmer. On April Fool's day, a heavy rain descended on northern Indiana, continuing for two days and nights. Nearby our home, the Tippicanoe River grew higher, wider and faster. Rumors reported that the river was over her banks.

My dad drove his 1923 Model T Ford to the river, allowing me, his five year old son to go along. Two miles north with many fields rain flooded, we came within sight of the river, an astounding picture. All the fields along the river were now river, causing the river to be ½ mile wide. My father had recently penned 27 ewes on a field that adjoined the river. That entire field was under water except for a small rise, a rounding of land about 60 feet in diameter, where the 27 ewes stood. He was surprised and immediately went to a close neighbor to borrow a rowboat. The neighbor was ill, but agreed to lend the boat. Dad loaded it into the Model T sideways and we hurriedly returned to the site of the sheep on the rise. He unloaded the boat, cut the fence and pushed the boat into the water. He took a roll of binder twine along and told me to stay in the car. He rigorously rowed to the sheep, perhaps 1/8 mile. Once there, he drove the boat onto higher ground. When he jumped out the sheep frantically crowded against the far water's edge. He cut several lengths of binder twine to tie their legs. He then proceeded to chase down the sheep, tie their legs and load them into the boat. He rowed them back to the Ford, hustled them onto the road in a heap, then went back to get more sheep, all in a sheet of rain. The ewes were heavy with lambs and soaked to the skin, weighing maybe 140 pounds or more. The second time was the same as the first, but the third, he had trouble with a factious ewe who tried the water rather than allowing him to grab her. Dad went in after her and drug her to high ground. There he tied her legs, drug her to the boat and rolled her in. Then he stripped his doused coat and wet overalls, which had so much water in the legs and pockets that he could hardly carry himself. Now he looked lighter in his under johns, a blue shirt and bald head, as his hat was now floating into a nearby field.

When he came to the road he wrestled the wet bodies to high ground, shaking a bit with the cold. He grinned his somewhat pearly teeth at me. He went back for the remainder in three more efforts attempting to recover excited ewes from a watery grave. He finally managed to get them back and unloaded. At this point, he was not a man in his winter underwear, but a muddy man, and even his bald head was a muddy pile. He tied the boat so it wouldn't float away, then drug and carried the soaked ewes into that Ford. He started the Ford and we chugged away to our home for our first trip home. Upon arrival, he pushed the sheep out, cut their bindings, and most of them got up and dragged themselves toward the barn. We made several trips. After the last trip, we ran toward the woodhouse. He dropped his muddy underwear, shoes and shirt to full nakedness and much mud. He called to my mother. She got all the hot water she had, which wasn't much, in a small bucket. My dad made a great improvement in front of the kitchen stove, thereby making a new man. Mom brought him another pair of long johns and the only other pair of overalls he owned. He literally collapsed and rested for an hour until noon. Then he hustled to get the barn chores done and the rain damage corrected.

The next morning we drove back to get the boat. There was no island and the boat was floating at the edge of the road. The water was across the road in many places. Dad brought

The Earl of Burton

a neighbor to help load the boat. He threw his wet clothes from the boat into the Ford and returned the boat to the neighbor. They talked for a bit and then he hurried home. He toiled all day washing the sheep manure and crud out of the Ford and taking care of rainy problems.

Three days later, all sunny and forgiven, he drove over to see how the river was acting. In the field where he had rescued the sheep, I was startled, as was Dad, who said, "Wow!" On top of the muddy and puddley meadow, which had just held 4-5 feet of water, there were hundreds, maybe five, six or seven hundred fish, wiggling and jumping and ready to croak. As a kid, who yearned to catch fish, and not too successful, I was spellbound. We turned the Ford around, chortled home, and got a tub and gunny sacks. We headed back to the river. My mother come along, after she first called Aunt May, Aunt Ruth and others to come. The fish were still jumping, but less alive, and we ran toward the fish with a bucket or sack. It was slick, and two times I fell down getting one ten inch fish. My dad and mom had slick problems too. They both had muddy legs, seats, arms and faces. We took home a tub and two full gunny sacks of fish. I didn't know or care what kind of fish they were, as this was phenomenal! Soon Uncle Lloyd came and brought Clyde Earl and Donna Mae. Aunt Mae came later as her 1924 Ford would not start for a while. Others were arriving too and it was a haul for all. It is unfortunate that cameras were not present. I saw many funny scenes, slipping and sliding as the fish were scrambling from one puddle to another.

Since it was too wet to work in the field for several days, the fish gatherers called for a fish feed. It was at noon the next day at Uncle Lloyd's house, since he had a good place to cook and feed many. Twenty nine neighbors came to devour fish, homemade bread and homemade butter. Aunt Ruth brought a two-gallon crock of pickled beets from her cellar, and these went well.

Now, after the big rain, the ewes were content in the sun. The fish had been the center of a great community feed and celebration, and I had time to think about my dad, who was something else. In years to come my admiration and zeal grew.

Note: By the middle of June we had 33 baby lambs who had survived the river flood. I'm sure the fat lamb sale helped our meager income.

The Milk Strike

During the late fall and early winter of 1930, my father and mother were more troubled than normal. Although I was only nine years old, I was aware of their increased sadness and perturbance. They went about their daily duties but they carried a great log on their shoulders. No one was sick currently, no animals had recently died, and I couldn't decide what worried them. I asked mom if the farm payment was due. She replied, "In January."

I asked, "Can't we pay it?"

She answered, "Yes, maybe we will make this one, but after that, no one knows."

My father was really down, and, although he relentlessly went about his work, I was sure he was sick or something dreadful. Often he took out a little black book from his front overalls pocket. He figured a bit with a stub of a pencil, sat in thought and then drove on. Often my dad and Uncle Lloyd huddled and talked and figured. Once four farmers came to our house and were in deep concern over figures. Now I had a hint. Dad called to mom to send the receipted milk figures for the last four months. She sent them with me and I delivered them to the men who sat in one of the automobiles because it was cold and snowing.

After this, Dad took numerous calls on the phone line, and Mom and Dad talked sometimes softly, and sometimes loudly. It had to do with the fact that the paycheck for the milk now was reduced to below the cost of the expenses. Our net income, what we had to exist on, was nil, even negative. To make the farm payment in January, he had to take the cash value out of his last life insurance policy. But his mortgage continued on. Now he had only $700 in the bank, but the payment was $1400.

It was rumored that the banks were failing. There were many essential costs in raising 40-50 milk cows, 10-15 horses, many hogs, chickens and the family - veterinary expense, medical doctor for the family, gas, groceries, oil, etc. And now Earl and Goldie felt the noose tightening around their economic necks. I wasn't too concerned, since my dad had always made it, but I worried a bit because they seemed to worry.

There seemed to be a plan afoot to try to do something about the milk prices paid to producers, and Dad and others seemed to have involved themselves. Quite a few phone calls on the party line preceded a meeting on a cold January morning as some 17 farmers in our area all congregated at Uncle Lloyd's farm. In four cars, they drove to Monterey, a milk collecting station where the Erie railroad picked up the milk from the milk trucks. There it was weighed, tested for bacteria and loaded on the train, which left at 9:15am sharp. It highballed to Chicago, arriving by 11:00am, to be processed, bottled, dispensed and delivered to almost two million families, groceries and outlets by 7:00am the next morning.

As my dad, uncle and the other four vehicles came close to Monterey, a small town on the Tippicanoe River, and beside the Erie railroad, they began to merge with other cars. The milk depot yard was filled with 150-200 farmers, all in working clothes and certainly without smiles. It was 8:30am and this day's milk must be loaded for this day's run by 8:45am. The men stormed the small office building and hurriedly advised the office manager to take a break

The Earl of Burton

and go fishing or whatever as they were in charge for a little while.

He was overwhelmed and yielded. A few men closed and locked the office while 150 milk farmers told the drivers of the trucks to unload them immediately. They rushed the dock and started dumping milk from the 400 ten-gallon cans. Where? Alongside the railroad. Four thousand gallons of pure milk, cooled, bacteria free, strained, ready to drink gurgled downwards and ran to a culvert, under the railroad and into the river. No milk for the people of Chicago from Monterey.

What the farmers knew was that this was a coordinated effort throughout the Chicago milk shed, all timed and executed in the entire area of Wisconsin, upper Illinois, upper Indiana and lower Michigan. All milk suppliers met the same fate and no trains delivered any milk to the people of Chicago. There were no milk unions or organizations, but ten leading farmers met with the milk buyers, and at 10:00am advised them that there could be no milk until the prices were negotiated. The mayor of Chicago exploded on behalf of his people. The president of the United States and other high officials asked the farmers to send the milk, while the government worked out a solution. The farmers asked for an immediate solution, as each day's delay would increase the pressure on themselves to submit. Few of the 100,000 milk suppliers could do without income for more than three or four days.

After a second day of dumping and threat of armed troops to oppose the farmers the Pure Milk Association was under horrendous duress and threats. They agreed to meet and settle the strike. At midnight, 84 farm leaders, 20 buyers and government officials at all levels hammered a 2 cents a gallon increase, making milk the same price as gasoline, 9 ½ cents per gallon. It was found that Pure Milk Association had been banking hundreds of thousands of dollars daily at the depressed price which had been grossly lowered in August. Now they would bank only half as much.

With the economic system failing the middle men were overprotecting themselves at the expense of collapsing farmers. The farmers were frantic for the other victims, the people of Chicago. But they felt they had to act until the middle men were squeezed into a corner and agreed to work on the same basis as the farmers.

Ninety percent of the regular milk supply returned to Chicago the next morning, and the party line system spread the word. The farmers had to subsist to be producers. President Hoover was overjoyed. An agreement had been reached and the farmers, including my dad were breathing easier, but actually the increase he managed to get from the strike was only 80 cents per day. The $31 a month he got was further reduced by the trucking company charges for hauling the milk. The milk farmers never struck again, and the prices were horrible for three years. Pure Milk Association put farmers on their board and kept their books open. With this new working system, every increase or decrease was known and accepted.

Economic Notes: My father bought his farm in 1923 for $80,000 after he and mother were married. Then he purchased a milk base, which is a contract with Pure Milk Association. He was indebted for the cows and the preparation of the buildings.

The depression crash came in January of 1929, and the ensuing struggle to stay afloat was unbelievable for all. In

The Earl of Burton

1932 the country, including my dad was ready to sink. After the local bank had closed its doors with $720 of his money, he could not pay his taxes. In desperation he applied for the job of driving the school bus route for the local elementary school, which picked up 20-25 students.

Fifteen very desperate people applied for the job. It was awarded to my dad. He had a monthly check coming of $65. However, he had to buy the truck chassis for the school bus. So he bought a Ford truck chassis for $410 and the township bought the bus. I don't know where he got the money to pay for it, but after repayment on that, gas, oil and tires, totaling maybe $15, he had $40 left to keep from perishing.

He also had another income. He received $5 for every colt that stood, suckled and was healthy from every mare bred by his stallion, Major de Hemmel. He was a stallion of great repute. Farmers from miles around came to have him sire their colts. This amounted to some $200 per year. While it dribbled in, it was money. Some farmers paid in grain, produce or even work, whatever they could barter. All in all, the impending crisis in our country was solved by such things as the milk strike and people like my father who played every angle and worked like dogs.

CHAPTER 3

Life on "Earl's" Farm

Feasting on the Farm.. 81

The Cellar.. 90

Wash Day 93

Our Barn.. 96

Feasting on the Farm

Did we starve during these times? You may judge from the following pages.

Pork - Hams, roasts, bacon, chops, cracklins, lard, tenderloins, pigs' feet.... Butchering hogs was quite different in my youth. In my day, we often killed and bled three to four 250-pound fat hogs every year. The hogs were gathered in a pen close to scalding barrels of hot water. There they were shot between the eyes, approximately an inch above their eyes. Then their throats were slashed with a sharp knife and they were allowed to bleed, drained of their blood. Immediately hereafter they were hoisted on a large block and tackle and put over the scalding hot water, which was in a steel barrel. The hog was dropped into the barrel from the block and tackle overhead, in and out, in and out, three to four times, until the hog bristles could be easily scraped by a scraping blade. Once the hog was cleaned of all bristles, he was placed on a large tin slab and all interior parts were carefully removed. The intestines were removed first. Then the feces was pressed out and flushed. They were carefully cleaned, turned wrong side out and scraped on a maple board. They were then sterilized with hot salt water, whereupon they were slipped on the casing spout.

As much as 10 to 15 feet of casings, ready for miscellaneous bits of pork to be ground in the sausage grinder, were then forced through the casing spout, seasonings were added and sausages were formed. Different types of meats created different types of sausages and even hot dogs, which was a special recipe. The heart was saved and Mom's special recipe for the heart and liver was a guarded secret. The remainder went into a miscellaneous barrel and later become cracklins. Hoisted on a long table, the dissection rapidly took place as pigs' feet were severed and stored in a bucket. The hogs' head was decapitated and one butcher stripped the head of small bits of meat, including the brains. Afterwards the tongue was stored in a large crock until the head meat could be made into the delicacy of head cheese, another secret recipe known by only a few. The pig tail was removed and sometimes it was tied to the rear of someone's overalls or dress and everyone had a big laugh! Finally the carcass was stripped of the front hams and rear hams and they were destined for special treatment.

Recipe #1 will provide the secret recipe for the sugar-cured hams. Thereafter the sugar-cured hams were hung in the cellar until the day of use. Next, the jowl or neck muscles were severed and cut in squares, later to be applied to recipe #2. Thereafter, the fat was stripped from the neck and other locations if it was excessive and cooked in a big iron kettle, put in the lard buckets and later cooked and rendered into lard. A 2/3-gallon lard bucket was filled and sealed for the basement until Mom needed a new bucket of lard. One after the other, spareribs were sawed and chopped. The roasts were sequestered and the tenderloins were taken. This was my favorite. Small squares of tenderloin were tied to fish poles with a string that hung in the hot kettle a short time until it was crisp and tasty was a real delicacy for the kids.

Now the work commenced as the dissections had to be cared for and doing so in cold weather was the key. The meat had to be eaten fresh wrapped or short-term frozen or salted to prolong edible quality. Mothers cooked and canned the meats after stripping them from the bones and it went to the cellar in quart cans.

The Earl of Burton

Dad had the recipe for pigs' feet. He was the only one at our house to eat them, as I always thought about where they had walked. He also made cracklins from the odds and ends, which he stripped from the bones, cut up into inch pieces and cooked in a big iron kettle. Finally he put them into the sausage press and squeezed the grease out, leaving a nice tasty tidbit, especially for the dogs and boys after drying. This was Bill's, (Dad's dog) winter feed.

Recipe #1: The Recipe for sugar cured hams and shoulders came from my Aunt May.

For 20 lbs. of meat - 1 pint of salt, 3 tablespoons full of brown sugar, 2 tablespoons full of pepper, and a pinch of salt peter. Mix the salt, brown sugar, pepper and salt peter together, place the meat and mixture on a large brown sheet of paper, and rub the meat well with the mixture. Be sure to rub the mixture into joints as well. Cover with brown paper and then with cheesecloth. Tie it with twine and hang from the small end down so it can drip. Let it hang for a month before using. It could keep until spring.

Sugar Cane - In the heart of our truck patch, my dad planted cane and it grew thick and tall and fast. By the first of September it was tasseled and ripe. Dad enlisted all of the help he could find and he could always find me! We took sticks and walked through the cane and bladed it; meaning we knocked all the blades off. In another 3 to 4 days, he took his foot cutter; a sharp blade clamped to his foot, and cut the cane in armload lengths, bundles. I and sometimes with help from my mom tied them. Finally, the seedy tassel was cut off and we loaded the cane in the school bus. Friday evening and early Saturday morning after milking we took the cane to Leiters Ford to the sorghum mill and cider press. This was an exciting place. A

100 or more stakes with numbers were set in a field and you were assigned a number and unloaded your cane and apples there. There were many trailers, a few trucks, one other school bus and a lot of kids. Every kid that came with his parents got a glass of fresh cider.

The mill had dozens of belts going from pulleys to gears to chutes to presses, draining the buckets as they crossed the scales to you. Today it could not happen. There were no safety devices and shields. They would have been sited out of existence. Also, they were probably a bit unsanitary, but they turned out cider by the thousands of gallons and sorghum in an endless stream. It was noisy and squeaky and I always liked it. I was very sorry when things got modern and it shut down. It was a landmark to the Alspauch Brothers. Somehow they weighed your cane and you got so many gallons of sorghum molasses and light golden molasses, depending upon the type of cane. We always got 12-gallon cans of light golden and 25 of sorghum. They were both delightful and loaded with iron and vitamins, although we didn't know about those things then. You could trade apples for cider and Dad usually took 10 gunny sacks of miscellaneous apples and got two 10-gallon milk cans of cider. The mill was a gathering place and many neighbors far and wide congregated here and we had many visits. My father had a line of farmers waiting to talk to him and we didn't get home until 1 o'clock. We met several trucks and trailers on our way home. Aunt May, Uncle Fred and Ida Katherine were among them.

The Truck Patch - The truck patch is a prodigious (meaning big) garden of vegetables. Dad grew the staples of our table. Early and late potatoes. He had a total of maybe ½ acre in row crop rows. Sweet corn had two plantings on a ¼ acre. String beans had 8 rows of beans on strings and supports and this amounted to a lot of fresh green beans and 50 to 75 quarts of canned green beans. Peas added 60 to 75 pint jars. Carrots dug and filled 3 to 4 bushels of carrots. Cabbages were headed before early frost and wrapped in paper and buried in the cellar pit. Cantaloupes and watermelons, just a few hills, as many neighbors just gave these to you. Pumpkins, about six vines, as well as pickles. Six vines would provide quite a few pickles. Strawberries - Dad's patch was probably 60 feet by 60 feet and ever bearing. He usually had a lot of nice strawberries. Dad planted all of his truck crops in corn planter rows so that he could tend them with horse-drawn cultivators. He was a good grower, but he always competed with weeds.

My Mother's Garden - My mother concentrated on flowers but she also grew (1) Lettuce - several successive growths coming on throughout the summer (2) Radishes - same thing, several successive growths coming on (3) Onions - little green ones and large sweet ones (4) Squash - 2 hills, lots of squash were provided here (5) Rhubarb - the whole end of the garden near the outhouse, for some reason it was very healthy rhubarb (6) Beets - for our summer table and canning, maybe 30 pints (7) Sweet potatoes - a row in the garden, stored in the pit of the cellar for the winter (8) Tomatoes were strictly for the summer table and canning by mom and other neighbors. My mom had a small garden, but it was plenty big with canning, washing, 3 kids, 3 meals a day, cleaning house, church work and more. Every other row was always planted in flowers.

Cherry Picking Time - We had 5 big cherry trees along our garden fence and they were a sight to behold in bloom time. Then in June, they turned red, loaded with sweet cherries, delicious for pies and cherry cobblers and just "eatin'"! They were a chore to pick, as only Dad could hoist high ladders, so we had neighbors pick and share - a gallon for them and a gallon for us. Even then we had too many and sold part of ours. Mom got neighbor women to help her can them. We had maybe 100 quarts of cherries in our cellar.

Grape Arbor - On the near side of the garden, Mom had a nice big grape arbor where you could sit on hot days. It was here that I remember her cleaning green beans and, once in a while, reading the paper. The grapes were Concords, big luscious grapes for the table or to take along when you went for a ride. Mom made lots of grape jelly and jam, maybe 50 pints and half pints.

The farmwomen canned everything and there were techniques to doing it successfully. My parents used to joke about Dad's presents to my mother. Whenever he went to a farm sale, and there were quite a few of them, Dad would buy glass jars and rubber sealers, which meant more work, also more food!

Almost once each summer, we took a trip to Southern Michigan, near Berrien Springs, which was near lake Michigan. I thought, at age 3 to 13, this was where all the peaches and Bing cherries of the world were grown. We would get someone to milk our cows, of course, and we would leave after milking about 7:00am Friday. We'd load the Ford with necessary camping gear and head northward some 85 miles to the land of endless orchards. When we got close and finally found a place to pick fruit and camp, it was exciting. Each year we camped by a little creek and lots of others came to pick and we met kids from Michigan, Illinois and even Ohio. The Bing cherries were large and very edible. We would bring back 3 to 4 cases of 24 pints of cherries and all the peaches the running board would carry, even 10-12 bushels, double high on each side. With the Ford overloaded, we had tire blowouts and overheating when we pulled big hills. One thing for sure, the quality of the peaches and cherries were excellent and upon coming home we shared with the neighbors and those who had helped Mom can for our cellar show.

Dairy Products - With 30 Holstein cows you can be sure that we had milk and cream and, with these, you can have healthy dairy products. I believe my mother continuously had a cheesecloth bag of cottage cheese on the clothesline. We always had a crank churn and cranking was an evening chore after dinner. We had more butter than we could use. We drank milk without remorse. Sometimes Mom would make other cheeses. Dad was generous with milk and gave it to the poor neighbors, the hobos, the gypsies, and to relatives. When Lloyd Reese, my uncle, worked for us, part of his pay was a gallon of milk, butter and cottage cheese every day or two.

Baking - From the crash of 1929 to 1935, my mother baked bread, as money was extremely scarce. Yeast sat on the stove shelf and a swollen pan of dough was ever ready for the next baking. As soon as we became less poor, she bought bread. We were all glad as we thought that this was a step up. Seldom did my mother bake rolls, but she sure could make tasty donuts and cookies and especially cobblers with cherries, peaches and apples.

Pickings - Huckleberries were abundant around about our neighborhood woodlands, especially down by Aunt Minnie and Uncle Orrey's house. In fact, their son, Ogden, as an adult, grew blueberries for a good living. It was some fun picking them out in the big woods, but they were small and the bucket filled very slowly, so I preferred to do farm work. We had no shortage of huckleberries and later blueberries, and I am still not sure whether blueberry pie or huckleberry pie is the best! Other pickings, such as gooseberry, raspberry and blackberry, were present. There wasn't much enthusiasm from this guy for gooseberries. Lee Moore and lots of others knew about Andy Gump mushrooms and morels, but my mom ruled them out as overall dangerous.

Beef Steak - I must not omit steaks, hamburgers and veal, since we had a good supply. We butchered a steer a year and sometimes more if a cow or bull failed. This was not quite as involved as hogs and Dad usually did this while we were in school.

The Art of Making Apple Butter - Since one tradition seems to be inspiring our family at the present, the art of making apple butter and applesauce, I thought all might like to hear how it occurred 70 years before. Aunt Sylvia and her family and Aunt Donna and her family usually joined together. They rounded up many sacks, crates or bushel baskets of the best apples and brought them to our house. Dad had a large copper kettle (or he had borrowed it, I'm not sure).

Dad built a rowdy fire and the first load of apples was peeled and cored. They were dumped into the boiling cider and the pottage was stirred in the hot copper kettle by a long-handled paddle. The paddle had a 10-foot or so long handle. A board fastened downward with holes bored in it and newly husked cornhusks tied through some of the holes. This enabled you to stir the big kettle to keep it from burning and sticking on the sides. The stirrer was usually

The Earl of Burton

an adult who had experience in cooking apples and making apple butter.

A batch of apple butter amounted to 7 gallons and often the cooking was repeated 3 times, so 21 gallons were divided between 3 families or however many took part. A pint and quart can of light red apple butter was a pretty sight on the cellar shelf. The reddening was made possible by dumping a pound of redhots into each batch.

Crusty apples were made and given to the kids. These consisted of taking especially good eating apples and dipping them into a pan of slightly over-cooked apple butter that had partially crystallized. The apple stem was tied or strung and dipped into the crystalline sauce, creating a special treat.

For applesauce the apples were cooked, but not boiled in cider. Sugar and redhots were added and an applesauce press was used to turn out the sauce. Some had a fitting that went into the meat grinder. The containers of applesauce were sealed and stored in the cellar. Now Sheri and Joe, does our applesauce equal or surpass the old days?

The Cellar

Our house had a 2-room cellar where we stored our root vegetables, canned goods, cured meats and lots of other things. And if a tornado ever came, we knew where to run. It had an outside entry and, until we rebuilt our house when I was 16 years old, the only way to the cellar was around the house and down the outside steps through flat doors and then inside doors. This cellar was a wonderful world. It had big earthen shelves around the room and wooden shelves above. Row upon row of canned fruits and vegetables, meats, jams and jellies and so forth told you we might be poor, but we had lots to eat. This was the family's store house. Most farmers had a cellar either under the house or nearby underground. I've been in many of them. Some were marvels - much classier than ours, but ours was good.

Aunt Ruth and Uncle Lloyd Castleman were more prosperous in the days when I was young and they ate like kings. Aunt Ruth had a hired woman to help her can and garden and Uncle Lloyd had a bigger truck patch than ours. But the difference was the cellar. It was cement. It was neat and clean, white-washed, snow white. There were vents to the above rooms so that they could cool their house on hot days. There were special bins and rooms to store roots and tubers. She probably had a thousand quarts of shining fruits and vegetables. They had a big Coleman light, powered by batteries. There were rows of sugar cured hams and shoulders and a straw and loam pit, where the carrots and other vegetables were stored.

We had maybe 500 quarts and many pints and half pints sitting on the big earthen shelves. They were dark spidery wood shelves, and we had to light the lantern to find

The Earl of Burton

whatever Mom sent us for. We had a potato bin so our potatoes never froze, even in a blizzard. Our cabbages, onions and sweet potatoes were all straw pitted. Our hams and shoulders hung proudly. There were rows of lard buckets, more rows of golden syrup, sorghum and honey, all marks of affluent eaters. In summer we would make ice cream in a big 2-gallon freezer and keep it packed in ice and burlap for 1 ½ to 2 days. Mom kept her eggs cool there in the summer. Dad kept his cow and horse medicine down there. I want you to know that if you haven't seen a farm cellar, you have a treat in store!

Note 1: With such a supermarket in our cellar, food we always had, but money to pay the farm payment, NO, NOT ALWAYS! Money to get anything new for the farm or the household, NO!

Note 2: Lois lived in town on Main Street among the notables and they had a similar food arrangement. Her grandfather had a big truck patch and Grandma Bell had a great garden. It wasn't often that you had to go to the grocery store.

Note 3: The Briles' family drove a Huckster Wagon in World War I and thereafter, first pulled by a team of horses. Later, I remember a very old Model T Ford Truck chassis with a box bed built thereon to hold a small store of groceries, cages for chickens, cases of eggs etc. Dale Briles had an "ooga" horn, which he worked as he approached our house every other Thursday. My mother had mixed reactions, as Dale had many items she wished for, but no money. If she wanted the item bad enough, she had to corner and catch one or two grown chickens to trade with. Dale Brials used bait to catch children. He gave a sucker for 10 cents of a bill that was expended. His prices were high, so most farmers' wives bought only necessities. I didn't like him because often we didn't even get a sucker. Still I had hopes when he honked.

Wash Day

Since the world of the USA washes clothes in an uncanny manner such that weather is no factor, it can be done quickly with the press of a knob, and dried without sunshine and wind, I think it might interest one and all to know the way it used to be done, at least on Earl's farm. Washing was a necessary drudgery.

My mother had 4 children. She was a slight woman, often ill and under constant work pressure from washing, ironing, drying and patching. She was a good seamstress but could only find time in the evenings, first under a kerosene lamp and late in the 30's under an Aladdin lamp.

My memory goes to our basic old farmhouse when we had to wash in the kitchen. The wood cook stove heated the water. It was poured by buckets and big pans into the wash tub. Lie soap was shaved and the Rub Tub was first used. This was too hard for me and often for Mom, so Dad tied his horses, came in and rubbed for a couple hours. Then he helped her put the overalls in the rinse water and together they rang them by hand.

The advancement came when Dad and Uncle Charlie cemented a porch floor to the back of our house. The roof did not come for many more years, but it helped Mom by keeping the washing out of her kitchen. Dad ran the pipe from the pitcher pump in the yard into the concrete and up with a faucet. I could then pump water into cold rinse water tubs. We got a ringer to squeeze water out of the clothes. It was only partially successful, but it was an improvement, except for the turning. This was bad for rainy days, snowy days or just cold ones as water on the cement froze and became slick. To cure that we scattered ashes thereon. My mother had to dress warm to offset the cold and her hands and nose were usually beet red. She managed – with the help of Dad carrying big buckets of hot water from the stove in the kitchen and my questionable help. I hated wash day. It just was no fun. When my mother was pregnant or was ill it was quite a problem. One time Dad hired an 18 year old German girl, Helga. She worked well but was not happy, as I recall, and stayed only until my mother had little brother Joe.

Finally, the Maytag came along and eventually my dad got enough money to have one. It had a gas engine that scrubbed the clothes and rinsed them and had an automatic roller to take water out. This machine had to be made in heaven and was greater to my mom than wheels. Only one problem. My mother had long hair that when unrolled reached to her ankles. She combed it once each day if she had time. She had it partially hanging from her head and was feeding the rollers with clothes when her hair got into the roller. It almost scalped her, but she hit the automatic release in time and only had a scare. She still had to hang clothes to dry on the clothes line and in cold weather the clothes froze. The frozen underwear and overalls gave you an idea of how many and how big the men and kids were in the family.

The Earl of Burton

A Depiction of Wash Day Drudgery
Woman unknown

Our Barn

It was:

1. The Farm Factory: Where some 100 cows, horses, pigs and Belgium's were stored, fed, watered, bedded, birthed and doctored.
2. The House of Great Stallions: Belgium's Major de Hemel, King Albert and Benjamin de Houtin and Jack, the mule stud.
3. The Milk Parlor: 32 Stanchioned Holsteins and Guernseys – calf pens, dry sack feed, mineral salt
4. Ensilage Storage: 33'X10' It was the finest known storage of green feed
5. Work Stalls: 8 for horses, 1 short stall for Pony, long racks of bridles, halters, lead ropes, collars, pads, sets of harnesses, curry combs and brushes, medicine

6. Feed and Loafing Shed: Young cows, Dry cows, cows off milk, chutes from the haymow shooting feed into feed sacks. Manure spreader storage. 3 sows furrowing, brought in from the cold.
7. Grain Storage: Corn crib for horse corn and close by a granary for great bins of oats, wheat, soybean, ground corn and mixes ground.
8. Barn Loft: It was a haymow, filled with alfalfa, clover and timothy for the horses. Mountains of oats and wheat straw – a heap of hay and bedding.
9. Milk House: Attached to the barn it contained tanks with stirring paddles as the milk had to reach 64 degrees to maintain a low bacteria count by 7:30am and washing equipment.
10. Equipment Storage: Animals came first, so the equipment often had to put up with snow and rain until good weather days came.
11. Cats: 10 permanent cats lined up in the milk house to have their tummies filled with streaks of milk, shot by Earl, "The Milker". The cats earned their milk, keeping the snakes (great king and rattle snakes), rats and mice under control. Their names? Itsy Bitsy, Splat Splot, Ish Kibble, Ish Kidabble, Mathew, Mark, Luke and John.
12. Chickens: Red roosters, Banties, and laying hens nesting in the haymow, all creating a raucous clucking, calling to someone.
13. Owls: Barn Owls – Hootin' and Cooin' to each other. Helping the cats keep the rats and mice under control
14. Pigeons: Lots of pigeons. I once thought I knew their language, but that was long ago.
15. Barn Swallows: On the edge of the roof, rows of clay nests. They were a nuisance, but Dad said they were good birds.

16. Basketball Court: In the haymow, whenever there was room, a basketball court was made. Hoops were attached to barrels and lots of days found the neighborhood boys on the haymow basketball court
17. Stockade: This huge exercise yard was attached to the rear of the barn. It was 200'X100'. For 1 hour, the stallions were let loose and ran like crazy. This was also the location of the "teasing" pole that was used to determine when the mares were ready.
18. Medicine/Veterinary Box: Found in the corner of the cow barn, this huge box contained home remedies, bandages, things left behind by the "real" vet – everything dad needed to help the "animals in need".

CHAPTER 4

Special Memories of "Earl"

The Bee Tree 101

Automobile Tales 104

The Indianapolis Bus Barn 108

Dexterity Too! 112

Wawasee Revival! 115

The Burton Church Picnic 119

The Gypsies 125

Crossing the Erie by a Hair 130

The Bee Tree

A custom that began in the early colonies and persisted until the depression made "Bee Trees" fair game. The custom was if a man found a hollow tree full of honeycombs and honey, he could cut the tree and take the honey provided he was brave enough to withstand the fierce onslaught of stinging bees. Another danger was that you might encounter an owner who had not heard of the custom. Nevertheless, my dad had an eagle eye for "Bee Trees". He always had a half dozen spotted. There was one on the Clayborn property, which he watched for 3 to 4 years. He first saw it when we rented and farmed the property. We later ceased to rent the property, but Dad's interest in the "Bee Tree" didn't cease.

Plans were made with Uncle Lloyd Castleman. On a moonlight night in October, when the temperature was nippy and the bees were at bed sleeping, we loaded Uncle Lloyd's truck with lanterns, cross-cut saws, axes, wedges, buckets, pans, tubs and a smoker. We had homemade hoods with screened wire outlooks. Clyde Earl, Uncle Lloyd, Evert, his hired man and I filled out the war party.

We coasted to a stop on a lonely road and handed the equipment over an old fence. After Dad and Uncle Lloyd sized up the tree they set the cross cut and started eating through the 3 foot rotten oak tree about 8 feet below the bees' domain. Clyde Earl and I lit the lanterns and put on our hoods. Evert didn't have a hood to protect him. We could hear the bees as they growled at our saw vibrations with a humming noise.

Dad yelled for us to get back and get ready to charge the tree with ladles and buckets. It was our job to gather the broken honeycombs and running honey. When we were set, Dad took a wedge and drove it into the saw cut at the precise point that the tree was to fall. Dad and Evert then finished the job. They sawed rapidly and the great tree shuttered and leaned and finally gave up and swished the moonlight as it fell to a shadowy grave with a big "thump"! As it hit the ground, Clyde Earl, Uncle Lloyd and I charged the downed tree with lanterns, buckets and ladles. Sure enough, it was full of honey. The great hollow trunk split apart and gallons of comb and honey ran out on the ground. Dad scooped it up with buckets as I held the lantern. All hands were furiously busy salvaging every pint of these bees' work.

Within seconds the bees came out of their shock and began dive bombing the lanterns, men and I with furry. Our hands and legs got many little needle pricks that hurt like sin. Dad and Evert had no head stalls. The bees seemed to know this as they led a cavalry charge against their heads and faces. Dad stayed for another scoop of honey and then hastily retreated in the face of a thousand stingers. He set the honey down and ran and swatted like a windmill. He pulled on a head protector and put on a pair of leather gloves. He then lit the smoker and pumped it, yielding clouds of sulfur fumes into the air. Then he took the cross cut and sawed new openings into the hollow logs, setting new streams of honey free.

The bees continued their attack. However, with the help of the smoker, the heavy clothes, and the head protection, we won the battle. It was a battle that had lasted for hours and by the time we got the honey loaded and climbed back through the fence, we felt like celebrating. Instead, the

The Earl of Burton

millions of darts in our hides forced us to straggle home. There by the light of Uncle Lloyd's Aladdin lantern, we began picking out the bee darts. I didn't feel good and Dad was about done in. We washed the honey and went to bed.

The next morning, Dad took longer than usual milking as his hands were swollen. His face was swollen too and his eyes were partly closed. Mom pulled many more stingers from both of us. She pulled two big ones from Dad's seat. I didn't feel good for a couple of days. Dad said that was the price we had to pay for the biggest honey haul he had ever made. After the bee food was strained we had, as our share, 16 gallons of honey stored in the cellar.

Automobile Tales

From 1921 to 1930 we had one car, such as it was. It had no side curtains, was not rain proof and invited dust. There was no heater or air conditioner, just two buffalo robes to keep us from freezing. There was no starter. It had to be cranked, often with the headlights of a neighbor shining on the crank. There were carbide lanterns on the side.

The Essex - In 1930 my dad bought an Essex four door, enclosed car. It had glass windows and except for a few cracks in the floorboards, it let little air in. It had 4 doors which opened front to rear. Once we almost lost my mother as the front door came open. She reached to grab it and skidded onto the road. Fortunately dad had almost stopped when he saw the door fly open. After that he wired it shut with haywire.

That Essex was a smelly, devilish car. He could not keep it going. It refused to go in cold weather. When running, it smelled of musty oil. He had to carry a can of oil, stopping often to keep the oil level up. Water was the same way. When it started to steam, he had a milk can of water in the back seat from which he gave the radiator more water.

Why did he buy this? Because he had no money, it was enclosed (Mom's request) and it was dirt cheap. It looked O.K., I guess, but because it wouldn't start in the cold, we parked it in the barn, where it was warm. The pigeons roosted above it and decorated it with white spots. It burped – especially to start out after backfiring. I didn't like that car and I don't think it liked us. My mom was embarrassed when it burped loudly. In addition it was so noisy you

The Earl of Burton

could hear it coming for a mile, the springs were bad or nil and it rode like a wagon.

1924 Buick - Dad traded the Essex for a 1924 Buick that we were proud of. It had little vases on the interior walls for flowers, a little bit of class. It too had problems as someone in the past had abused it. In 1937 we bought a new Plymouth. Between those times, T's dominated.

Now at 11 or 12 years of age, my dad had instructed me to drive the Buick around the farm and short distances down the road to help him. One morning he told me to bring the Buick and pick him up down at the Mud Creek Farm. He then left, taking off with his horses. As he whacked his team with the lines, they started off at a fast clip. I had to meet him and bring him back so he could drive the school bus. At the Mud Creek Farm he tied the horses, knowing he would return soon.

As I was getting into the Buick two of our dogs wanted to go along with me. I told them to hop in and we headed for Mud Creek Farm. As I turned on the road, one dog tried to get on my lap and the other was licking my cheeks. I shoved them off and tried to get the Buick going straight down the road. In a wink, the Buick got off the road, rolled across the fence, did a complete summersault and landed on its wheels. I was in shock but was OK. The dogs were crying. My mother came running, thinking I was torn into ribbons. She solaced me, then remembered dad's bus and ran to the party line. She called my Aunt Donna at Mud Creek Farm. The next thing I knew Earl had unharnessed one of the horses, jumped on his back, whipped him hard and was galloping down the road toward our house. Seeing the scene and the Buick in the pasture, he tied the horse, ran to me and looked me over. He then ran to the Buick and looked it over. He got in it, tried starting it and it worked. He ran it out of the pasture, across the pasture and into the barn lot. He then jumped out, ran to the school bus and roared out – just 10 minutes late.

In high school, I took up basketball. Getting back and forth to basketball practice and games and not interfering with the milking, was shortening my leash because we had just one car. Dad found an old ford in a barn, gave it me as a gift and we became a two-car family. I named it the Mayflower. I remember we often shuttled neighbors and friends.

My two sisters also existed on this car resolution. Dad and my mother never complained of the taxi duties.

The Jitney - Now what is a jitney? The one I recall was my father's school bus. When he hauled kids it was a school bus. When he hauled everything else, it was a jitney. As a jitney, it carried sugar cane, potatoes, calves, implements or destitute families and their belongings.

Just to let you know the legal ownership and origin I opine as follows: My dad was the lowest bidder on a public offer to provide a school bus for our rural route. He retained that route for 12 years. He bought a new chassis and truck and during the season of school, bolted a school bus body thereon. As soon as school was no longer in session he was at liberty to use his truck at will. In early years he continued to use the school bus during the off season. The contract simply said that he must keep the body in good repair. Then, about 5 years later, he got a truck bed. From this point on the school bus body was bolted on the chassis during the school year and the truck body was bolted on the chassis during the non-school season. First, it was a Model

The Earl of Burton

T truck. Later he replaced the Model T with a bigger and stronger ford truck.

I believe this would be frowned on today and while I doubt that this was all legal, my father never knowingly violated the law and/or there were few officers of the law hovering about Burton.

The Indianapolis Bus Barn

It was customary in our community to let the school bus drivers bid for specific routes within the school district. The school district provided the bus body and the driver provided his own motorized chassis. A Trustee of the school district put out bid specifications on March 1. My dad figured long and hard, based on past experience, as he had just finished a 2 year stint as a driver. During that time he had rented Dee Barrier's truck and now Dee wanted his truck for his own use. The bids were published and Dad received the South Mud Creek Route at $2,880.00 per year for 4 years with a $40 annual increase. The catch was that he had to buy a motorized chassis, which he bought at Lauderbach Chevrolet for $470.00. Mom wondered out loud whether $279 per month was enough to offset the loss of time in the fields, but Dad said this was 1929, milk prices had just dropped terribly and this was <u>real dollars</u>. We had 2 days of rain, which kept Dad from plowing. The Trustee called asking him to pick up the new school bus body and take it to The Indiana Bus Company Barn in Indianapolis, where it would be fastened to the chassis. It was April 18th, 1921.

For once my dad asked me to go with him. I was 8 years of age, a year beyond a year of pneumonia. This was a treat for me - a day away from school and being with my dad. Dad picked the chassis up at Lauderbach's. I was chilled by the site. It had no windshield, no seat except a gas tank to sit on, and no floorboards. This would be no fun on cold or rainy days or after a mile or two on any day. Dad framed in a piece of glass in front of the driver and fastened a cushion to the gas tank. He put in some floorboards so I wouldn't fall through. At 7 o'clock on April 18th, after milking a bit

The Earl of Burton

early, Dad tied me on with a rope. Mom gave me my gallon lunch bucket for snacks. Dad said we would eat in Indianapolis. The day was gray and I soon scooted down under the dash to avoid the wind as we headed for the bus factory. We went via Michigan Road, State Highway 25. Despite my cramped quarters, I watched to our rear and in this "fresh air" truck we traveled on a mighty trip of 100 miles. We passed through Logansport, then through Burlingame, Michigan Town and Kirkland. We got gas at the outer edge of Indianapolis and by 11 o'clock we drove into the bus factory. I was cramped and excited about seeing a big city. However I was a bit undecided and apprehensive when we found the bus factory in the midst of "Negro town". Black people were everywhere. This was my first exposure. Black men sat on cement walls across the street from us in great numbers, evidently without a job and black women and children seemed to come along regularly.

Immediately across the street was a restaurant. I think that since I had never gone into a restaurant, nor eaten in one, what I saw was a bit disappointing. My dad said it was a diner, which is a small restaurant. About 12:30 he took me across the street to the diner. My interest diminished the closer that we got to the door. There were at least a dozen black people towering around me and Dad. I would have run away except for Dad. He lifted me into the doorway. Abruptly a shot was fired and some dropped to the ground. My dad grabbed me and ran into the street, as fast as traffic would allow, then back to the bus factory. He was frightened and my dad didn't get that way often. People scattered up and down the streets and a small black man with a sock cap pulled over his face with slits cut out for eyes looked both ways and ran down the street, through the traffic and disappeared into an ally behind a big building.

Even before he disappeared, policemen came on foot and in cars with sirens screaming. The police went in the diner, then came out, looked and left. I was still hungry, but not for the diner. Dad talked to the man working on our bus. He told him to take the streetcar 7 blocks south to a little restaurant. I liked the streetcar ride, but cannot remember what I ate or much about the restaurant. I do remember a lot about the diner.

When I was permitted to enter our school bus, I was really pleased - the shiny windows and cushioned bench seat, all air tight and it smelled quite new. I rode in style, trying every seat on the way home. I watched the countryside slide by. By the time we drove into our sandy lane at Burton, I was feeling very proud of our new bus, my dad the driver, and that I lived in Burton town. My mother came hurrying out carrying baby sister, Muriel, and running ahead was sister June.

Note 1: Dad drove the bus some 11 years and the kids liked Earl and they always gave him Christmas notes that they had written. My recollections of my dad's tenure as a driver was a team of horses tied to post with Earl running to get the bus. He would take the kids home, then go back to the horses for another hour or more of work. On winter mornings dad milked early, from 5 to 6:45 a.m., started the bus for it to warm up, strained the milk into the big 10-gallon cans and then drove the bus route through snow, rain, sleet or whatever. When the motor would not start, he harnessed a team of horses. He called my mother to drive the bus as he pulled it with the team.

The Earl of Burton

Obtained Indiana Bus Company

The New Schoolbus

The old School Bus
Burton School in Background

Dexterity Too!

The Pole Squirrel - God created squirrels and other critters, permitting them to climb trees and hide themselves, food and other things. Man created telephone lines and poles to hang them on. Burton community had to keep their lines open themselves. Often someone had to climb a pole and correct difficulties. There were pole climbers in Rochester, but they were costly. Several young neighborhood men in their teens tried to meet the challenge by becoming pole climbers. Only three or four of them got to the guide arms. When they climbed, they had a heavy leather waste band. It was a thankless job, but three of them practiced until they were good enough to handle the job. They took turns obliging Bartley who was the line operator of the telephone company. Then one of the teens went away to the army, the other two got too busy and still a pole climber was needed.

Earl Mathias became the guy that squirreled up the poles. There was no payday, just appreciation. One took note of the guy who fled up the tallest silos, skirted high places and if you had heard of his identity, twas the same one that skidded up the phone poles. I don't know when he gave it up. But I know I went on to become an athlete, but I could never climb that darn telephone pole. I had several scars and stickers on my belly to show I had tried. I introduce you to my dad, the pole climber.

The Silo Ring - As my dad set the ensilage cutter, locked the tractor and tightened the belt to the supply power we knew fall was here, an exciting time. Dad connected a string of 8 to 10 inch pipes 30 feet in length. He climbed the silo at the doors with a rope around his shoulders,

The Earl of Burton

connected to the pipes. As he reached the top, he scooted around the top, riding a narrow cement or wood stave of two or three inches. He scooted around the perimeter to an extension where he could hook on, pull the row of pipes upright and fasten them securely with a chain. He then attached a series of pipes 20 feet down into the silo. All this I watched as I had ascended behind him, holding tight. I watched my dad in this intricate maneuver. I also took this time to scan the horizons far away. From 30 feet in the air, a rare opportunity, I saw that down below there were little trees, the pastures, little cows and Uncle Lloyds barn. I could see far away, perhaps ½ mile and I scanned the horizons looking and wondering. Before we went back down I saw a passenger train ½ mile away whistling for Loyal.

Silo filling is both interesting and smacked with a bit of danger. Every fall in Indiana and other Midwest states newspapers report of nasty and disastrous injuries at the hands of the ensilage cutter. My dad had a 50% interest in ours. He was the operator and get-up man and as usual, the "expediter". The practice was a successful way to store crops. The corn, stalks and other growings were chopped by the cutter. Then the bits were blown into the pipes and up the high silos, where they dropped far down inside the silo. There they were stomped by three or four men, removing air pockets. This new product was called ensilage. In the winters it was distributed to great Holsteins.

I inherited Dad's cat skill to scale the silo. In the winter I usually got the job of throwing down the ensilage, often prying it loose as it was frozen, but always to the delight of the Holstein mouths.

The silo ring assembly rotates, often filling ten or twelve silos. It is a satisfaction when completed by all owners. My mother was always very relieved that there had been no accidents at the completion of the final silo filling. The danger today has been eliminated by modern field choppers and storage, 75 years ago unknown. My mother's questions resonated "Why must my husband assume most of the danger for 12 members of the ring?" I think it was because he had the sole quality of willingness, always wanted to get the job done and was responsible.

If you want a job stomping, bring your raincoat and hat. For a dollar a day you can tromp in a 30 foot radius circle in a 30 foot high silo for 8 or more hours. Don't forget to be cheery when you get home and greet your wife. I've been in that job for just 2-3 hours at a time. It was easier, as I was young, but I always desired to be elsewhere.

For further information the writer has an article on a silo filling where a great disaster occurred.

Wawasee Revival!
~1935 - 14 yrs~

Phone – 3 rings 2 short – That's us. It's Saturday afternoon 1934, a crisp November day. Dad is just pulling in the lane after husking a big load of corn. Mom answered and they asked for Earl, so she quickly called to him as he was driving in. He tied his team, ran to the phone and was flabbergasted to be talking to Mr. Billy Sunday – one of the world's great evangelists. He was seeking to have Dad come sing at Wawasee Tabernacle on Sunday.

Who could refuse Billy Sunday? Dad accepted, agreeing to arrive by noon Sunday, tomorrow. This was exciting! Billy's top solo singer was ill of the flu. He was told of a local man, Earl Mathias who sang in a Rochester church, and thought him to have a fine voice. So it was to be!

My mother had serious eye redness and could hardly see. Sister June had stubbed her toe badly and could hardly walk. So Dad said he and I would go. I was always ready for an excursion.

Dad got up Sunday at 4:00am, got the cows in, fed and milked 28 cows. He called me at 5:30am. I stumbled to the barn, milked 3 cows, then got Queenie, my dog, and took the cows to pasture. Dad cooled the milk. He then went on to do lots of chores with hogs, Mom's chickens, and the studs. By 7:00am I arrived back from taking the cows. We ate Post Toasties, washed and put on our Sunday clothes. Mom and baby Joe, hobbling June and little Muriel bid us goodbye. We leaped into the Essex and took off in a cloud of oily smoke, heading for Wawasee to meet Dr. Bill Sunday!

We often drove the Essex, when it was willing, as Dad had given up on our old model T Ford. He brought the Essex out as it was enclosed and not as cold to ride in in cold weather.

We got to Wawasee by noon, located the tabernacle, and met The Billy Sunday, which was great. He patted me on the head and asked if I could play baseball. I said, "Sure, but rather feebly!" My father and he laughed and he said he'd like to play catch with me! Dad put a bear skin rug over the engine of the Essex. Then we washed up and viewed the Tabernacle. It was a sight! As we approached, we saw a very big round building that had most of the frame supports on the outside. Dad said they held the roof up so that the inside was 100% free of posts. Inside there were almost 2000 seats, all polished highly and with arms. Especially new to me who only had an outhouse, there was a great toilet with 6 porcelain seats and a pull chain to flush water down. I liked the mirrors to comb by.

There was an 1/8 mile lawn in front that sloped down to the sparkling lake of Wawasee. It was now cold and no swimming! Brrrr! Chilly, but I thought of going in. Then Dad called my attention to the figures, 10x life size, of Jesus accompanied by an angel on each side, descending on a stairs from the roof as if from Heaven to join us in the Tabernacle. Later, Mr. Sunday gave a very cordial invitation to Jesus to join us.

Inside Dad and I were given a sandwich and apple and we could have coffee. Then Dad practiced with a man who was to accompany him on the piano. They practiced until they got the music cinct. Then he found a seat for me, as it was almost 12:30pm. The Fords and Chevys were arriving in the field in front. The cars were parked and people filed in to be seated.

The Earl of Burton

Wow! I had a good view of the people coming in. The men almost always had white shirts and ties with hats – felt – in black and brown. They looked sharp! The women wore nice clothes but their hats were something – big brims and sometimes feathers and paper flowers sitting on top. My mom had such a hat, as that was the style. There were quite a few kids also and they, as well as I, got fidgety before the 3 hour preaching was over. I never saw so many dressed up people in one place.

Soon a pipe organ began. Dad had told me about its big, resounding tubes up to the ceiling. It was something. A lady told me, "This is God's music!" It resounded over the huge gathering and I told Mom about it when we got home. Initially, Dr. Sunday and ten men marched in together. My dad was with them. The crowd sang "Holy, Holy, Holy" as they marched in and were seated on the platform. Most of the ten men were other ministers, there to give pep talks, lead the prayers or they were musicians. A trumpeter bugled and Dr. Billy Sunday rose and said, "Hello!" My dad said he had converted 2700 baseball players and I looked for them, but sure could not tell. He was a handsome man, athletic, with a booming voice, an engaging smile and he sure did like the Lord.

Quickly my dad was introduced as a man God had given a voice and Earl used it for Him! My dad rose, stepped forward and the piano started. I could see that he was a bit nervous. His balding head was shimmering, his pearly teeth shown as he smiled and his large Roman nose shown as his soothing tenor voice – maybe untrained, but fetching began to sing. He presented "Ivory Palaces" in a clear and strong voice. I thought he did good, but I was unsure until 2000 people applauded loudly and held on for a long time. After

Billy's talk, and near the end, he was again presented. He really was good on "Whispering Hope!"

Afterward he stood in line with Billy Sunday and was showered with praises. I stood close and was proud! I don't think we came away richer in money as this was for God, but Dad whistled and talked jovially on the way home.

I didn't know things like this existed. Although I got edgy in the big sermon it was a power moment and I couldn't think of sleeping. Near the end Billy presented a picture of the devil and explained who he was. He asked how many had him often on their back and digging into their minds and souls. Almost 2000 hands went up. Soon he asked all those really having trouble with the devil – anger, fighting with wife or neighbor, guilty of cheating, stealing and not even asking God's forgiveness to "Come on down" and he would send that bird out of their lives. Soon 50%, I believe, came down the aisles and gathered to pray on their knees as Billy administered the Lord's Blessings. I thought, but really didn't feel the devil was on my back right now, so I sat very still.

We left about 4:30pm. Luckily the Essex started and we roared off. Billy Sunday said he wanted to play catch with me, but 2000 people also wanted to talk to him and we had to leave. Dad added oil and water and had one flat going home, but we made it by 7:00 pm. The cows were bawling loudly. Someone had brought them home from the pasture. We hurriedly hugged mom, the girls and baby Joe. Then we changed clothes and as usual Dad milked 25 cows and I milked 3. I then fed Queenie and Dad let me go to the house. He arrived by 9:00pm and we had a late supper with lots of talk. Maybe now my Dad would be famous. A Day to Remember!

The Burton Church Picnic

My ages were 5 through 10.

At last, the day of days had arrived, Sunday! But more than that, it was the day of the church picnic. For weeks, kids and everyone who went to church and a few who only went to the picnic, had this event on their calendar. On Saturday, Mom cooked her cookies and planned swim outfits for her, Dad, and me. Baby June was a bit too small. Since the Sunday School classes met on the banks of the river at 9:30am, we hurried to get the chores done and the Ford loaded. We left on schedule for once and headed for the Tippecanoe River, Trails End. As we came closer, our car joined a line of other Fords and a few Chevrolets. The lane back to the river was dusty. Mom placed a blanket over the baby and herself.

Shortly we parked in a beautiful tree studded meadow bordering the fine old Tippecanoe, a river of joy! As several cars and two trucks had arrived quite early, the setup was about done and binder canvases were hung around homemade toilet seats for the girls and a trench for the boys. The church was about ready with benches and pulpit. The huge picnic table, about 100 feet long was set up. And what a sight the soda pop was, all stacked high! Never had I seen so much and today they said it was free (orange, lemon-lime, grape, strawberry and lemonade by the glass).

Kids boiled out of cars with shouts of greetings and then a dash to explore. The river shimmered in the morning sun as it rippled along. WOW!

The minister, Reverend Roudebush, rang the hand bell and told us where each class would meet. Our teacher met us on the river bank. About 15 to 20 boys studied about Moses and the Nile River. I figured that river beat the Tippecanoe. How terrible it was that the pharaoh tried to kill all the boy babies, but we were glad the Princess hid Baby Moses in the bull rushes along the river. Harold Hoge said his dad would have shot anyone who tried to kill his baby brother and we all agreed, ours too. Our teacher, Mike Eash, made us appreciate the Bible, but today we were glad when the class was over so we could run for ten minutes before church started.

Church gathered at 11:00am. There were a lot of benches filled, many sat on the grass and several men elected to stand. About 150 people were present. All heard a sermon by Reverend Roudebush, who called for all to account for their sins. It was a fiery sermon and several came forward to be baptized and/or reclaimed. At the end of the sermon, some 10 were submerged; head and all, in the river. Prayers were shouted aloud and then privately.

We not only heard a devil chasing sermon, but we heard my Dad sing. I thought he was the greatest! He had a strong tenor voice that carried through the trees. He was accompanied by my mother on the harpsichord. Everyone seemed to like this and said "Amen"! Dad's first song was <u>Ivory Palaces</u> and the second was <u>Whispering Hope</u>. WOW!

It was 12:30pm and we were hungry. The dinner came alive in minutes as dishes popped out of cars and onto the table. I walked around the table and never saw so much food. I saw Aunt Minna's strawberry pie and Mom's beef

The Earl of Burton

and noodles. Then Uncle Ora said the blessing and I about got crushed in the rush.

My mom believed that your food would act like a rock in your stomach and you would drown if you went into the water too soon after eating. I never believed that because I never saw it happen, but that was the law. We put on our swim suits, an old cutoff pair of overalls. This was far more than I wore at the creek, but I did not have 150 people watching. We scouted the swimming holes, watched fish and crawdads and bragged to each other about how good we could swim.

Lee Moore came and acted as lifeguard. He yelled, "The last one in is a chicken"! He had a real swim suit with a shiny brass buckle on the belt. I hoped that someday I could have a suit like that. Today we plunged in and the sandy bottom felt good to our toes. We promptly had a splashing contest. Soon a lot of young men were in the swimming hole. They showed off their best swims and dives and contested who could hold their breath the longest while they sat on the bottom. They also swam far out into the river, where there was a long rope tied from an overhanging limb. They would swing out on it and drop in a deep hole. I was too little to go there, but vowed I would make it someday.

Next the dads came and this was a thrill. Decked out in old overalls and no shirts, their white long legs, arms and shoulders seemed whiter than snow, but they were welcomed by their kids. My dad rarely ever went swimming because he always had to work. He and other dads formed a locked hand platform and tossed me and a line of kids high like cannonballs. Some dads tried to do the tricks that they did when they were young unmarried men.

They were awkward compared to the young men like Lee Moore, Bill Baldwin, and Clyde Earl.

Up the river a separate swim was happening, made up of little girls, older girls and moms. Sometimes grandmas joined and I saw my mother carefully working down the slippery bank, testing the water with her toes. She finally moved into the water, submerging all but her beautiful crown of hair stacked on top of her head. If her hair was to get wet it would give her lots of trouble. Her swim suit was nice, a pair of bloomers with a short dress that was getting old on top. I always thought it was too bad I didn't swim with Mom too.

The cheering section was made up of those too old or too sick or too chicken to come in. Everyone cheered when Uncle Will came down the bank. He didn't look like Farmer Will without his round steel glasses. Little by little, most everyone could not resist the fun and body cooling pleasures and joined the brigade of those riding the Tippecanoe's back.

After the swim, most hit the ice cold pop tubs and selected a cold orange or grape. This was a very popular spot and the pop openers were busy. I tried all the flavors. Before we went home, I had a tummy ache and had to visit the binder canvas toilet to heave up some of that pop. I decided I'd stick to orange in the future. Then the games began. Me and Nelson Anderson won the sack race, although we all fell down twice. I liked Bible People, but Ida K won since she was older and smarter.

For the young men and old men, one of the highlights was a tug-o-war. Jim Mathias had found a muddy hole in the road. About 20 men took sides on the rope, the adult class versus the young men's class. Finally, the young men pulled Ross Moore and his men's class into the mud.

Another game I liked, but couldn't do, was the rope climb. Two ropes were hung from a tree branch and a $1.00 bill was tied at the top of the rope. Doc Miller, who worked on the railroad, was the only climber that climbed the rope and claimed the dollar. Several almost made it, but wore out. One dollar was lots of money, a day's wages.

Horseshoes were popular. My dad brought the shoes, because he had Belgian horses and they had big feet and the game needed big shoes. One contest was for the husbands and wives. It was a calling contest. Judges determined whose calling carried the furthest when Hubby called wife and vice versa. There was a prize for both the meanest (really nasty) and the sweetest voice. Twelve signed up and judges were selected. My dad was the loudest. He could yell. I can tell you as he yells at me ½ mile away. Dee Berrier was the sweetest and he was!

The games had to be cut short as the homemade ice cream was brought in about 4:30pm and at least 10 gallons of home-tested flavors were unpacked. The young men ladled it out as long as there were comers. What a way to END THIS DAY! My dad went back several times. I think I got my taste of ice cream from him. I wonder where they got that much ice. Granddad Mathias had an ice house and each winter they sawed chunks of ice out of his pond and filled the house. These cold quarters were double walled and sawdust packed, so part of the ice for the picnic probably came from there.

About 5:30pm my dad started thinking about cows to milk and ordered our crew to load up. Everyone hated to leave, but Fords were cranked and kids counted. Away we went in a cloud of dust, looking back through the ising class window in the rear of our Ford. I saw old Tipp as we went around the bend and in the evening sun she was still gorgeous. WOW! WHAT A DAY!!

The Gypsies

The faithful party line gave us advance notice! Horses and two wagons of gypsies were about ½ mile east on our road and coming at a trot. My mother was electrified as they were not her favorite people. I was 8 years old, Sister June was 4 and Muriel was 2. Immediately, my mother began fortifying the fort. She fed her chickens and got them in. She asked me to put up the barbed wire gate and wire it tight going into the barn lot and she called Aunt Mae to see if Earl was ready to come home. He was already on his way. Very shortly we heard them coming as they had bells on their harness. Mom made us all come in and she pulled the blinds and blocked the doors with chairs. She hoped they would think we were not home.

Sure enough, they pulled into our sandy lane. We watched them from the upstairs window. They unloaded seven people, two men, two women, and three children from 8 to 10 years old. Their clothes set them apart from any group. The men wore baggy pants and puffed sleeve shirts, where it is said they put their stolen items. Their hats were small maroon Fez's, straight from Turkey. The women wore very unusual garb and moccasin shoes with pointed toes and a bell at the tip. They wore long puffed silk bloomers and gay colors. Added to that were long silk lingerie robes with opportunity to show their breasts and jewelry. They adorned themselves with bangles, beads, bracelets and rings. Instead of one ring, like my mother, they would often wear eight rings. Makeup was applied heavily. To us, they looked and smelled very strange. These people had swarthy dark tanned complexions. It was said that they were from Romania or Turkey. The women wore a black spot on their foreheads. Their long flowing black hair was highly polished. They were very attractive and it was said that they were used as the bait to set trap. The children were miniatures of the adults. They ran and flitted around, checking everything out. It was said that the children were trained carefully in making slight of hand and identifying the contents of all buildings.

My mother's plan might have worked, but Dad and his team came down the road at a trot. You would have thought he was overjoyed to see them. They shook hands, patted backs, etc. Dad untied the barbed wire gate and drove his team into the barn lot. He had them drive in also. They watered their horses and in return gave him a couple of gifts. One was a braided lead strap that they had made. The other was perfume for his wife. Dad was a softy. He took them into the milk house where we had two gallons of milk, which he gave to them. The stage was set. They talked about horses, bragging about theirs. In particular they boasted about their beautiful Chestnut Sorrel. She had a long flowing white mane and tail and four white feet. According to them, she had not been broken to ride or drive. Dad tried to get close to her but she was frightened and did not want a man to touch her. This was a challenge to Dad, as he was a man who could train all horses. The mare's name was Zoalate and they said she was three years old. It appeared she had been abused. Only after running ropes around her were they able to get close. She snorted and her eyes rolled and danced. The gypsies threw the book at Dad. Within 20 minutes Dad owned Zoalate, having traded a two-year-old bay work colt and $4.50. They managed to get Zoalate in our barn with great difficulty.

The women were now at bat. They had retreated to their ornate wagons while the men dealt with Dad. Now they were fresh and beautiful. They began with inquiries about

The Earl of Burton

his family, ancestry, prosperity and indebtedness. Soon he took them into the kitchen. As he opened the door and invited them in, he was hit by 50 daggers from my mother's eyes. She retreated, gathering all three of her kids to her as if they would kidnap us. Dad called her in and the gypsy lady soon realized she was not going to make it with my mom. She concentrated on Dad. The gypsy lady sat at the kitchen table, asking my dad to sit on her right around the corner. She spread her silk coat to reveal her full bank of bangles. Showing quite a bit of her breasts, she leaned toward Earl Mathias and whispered something to him. He was flustered and in the grasps of a beautiful gypsy. She took a polished dagger from her garments. She placed it between herself and Dad, asking him to concentrate on the polished reflection of the dagger. She spoke in English with a heavy Turkish accent. She droned on to my father, repeating often wherein she said he was a good man, destined for a better life, which would soon be rewarded.

Earlier he told her he owed $16,500 on our place. She told him about 180 acres in north central Michigan, using words to paint a very graphic picture. There was a 20 acre lake, 50 acres of good timber and 100 acres of open ground for meadows, corn and other grains. The home was a large brick home with nice furniture, inside bathroom and heat. The barns were good. There was a village 7 miles away. For this they would do an even trade for our 120 acres with very poor buildings, very shabby and our debt of $16,500. She explained the place had been deeded to them by a man on his death bed who loved gypsies. However gypsies cannot be confined, but they know of a man who would buy such a farm as ours. *THE BOOT*: Major de Hemel, my father's intelligent Belgian stallion. He was widely known as the most valuable thing on this farm. At this point she drew my dad close and whispered again. They would permit him a trip to Michigan to check the property. He then would have five days to accept. And if not accepted, they would carry out the dagger's instructions, poverty and unhappiness! If, on the other hand, he accepted he would be rewarded. Her eyes were sensuous.

My dad was a common farmer whose moral code was set by the church, community and family. He was sweating as he was being tempted greatly. The gypsy lady sensed my father's consternation and quickly came to his rescue. She took the pearl handled dagger, razor sharp on one side and flat on the back side, and suspended it between two chairs. She marked prosperity on the north chair and hardship on the south chair. She explained to my father that all he had to do was spin the dagger. This he did and it spun and slowly died with the blade due north - Michigan! This scene, taking place at our spartan kitchen table was witnessed by my mother listening through the wall and three little kids crowding around her. We peered into the kitchen, wondering why our Daddy was with that strange woman and why we could not run to him. My dad agreed to give his answer to them at noon tomorrow.

Between that afternoon and the next day at noon the gypsies made several small deals and, in each case, my dad was the one to gain. They parked overnight in our woods and Dad took me to their camp fire they had kindled. We were close, maybe a bit too close, and they smelled funny!

Note 1: I think the gypsies made one mistake; that being asking that Major de Hemel be part of the deal. Major de Hemel would no longer belong to my father. This he could not do - King Albert, yes, or Benjamin, but not 'OLD MAJOR".

The Earl of Burton

Note 2: The wagon home of the gypsy family was about the size of a covered wagon, but much better furnished. It had a small coal burner, excellent slung beds with goose down bedticks, clothes storage and even Persian rug runners on the floor. Wood carvings were around the entry and food and trade items filled numerous outside drawers. The pin striped wheels were gay and painted in enamels to fit classy people - GYPSIES.

Note 3: Due to Dad's welcome, we had a visit most every year from a gypsy caravan, but nothing like the time we almost lost Major de Hemel.

Note 4: The gypsies' reputation as thieves, reprobates, horse cheats, and legal liars was well established. To this extent, when warned by a party line, some farmers caught a chicken or sometimes a pig and, when the gypsies came, they offered this outright if they would proceed down the road and leave the household in peace and safety.

Note 5: It was a traveling rumor that when a gypsy really took a local to the cleaners and it was heard about in the next county, it was because the women were used as bait. The victim would stay the night in the chambers of the gypsy wagon. Fortunately, I never heard of this in our neighborhood.

Crossing the Erie by a Hair

In summer and fall we went to Rochester almost every Saturday evening for a social and small shopping spree. Farmers that didn't have cows to milk got around early and went to town around 4:00pm. They got a good parking place on Main Street. The choice locations were between Wyle's Department Store and the Char Belle Theater. We never arrived until 7:30pm or 8:00pm due to cows and milk that had to be cared for. Hence, we usually had to park in an alley or on a back street. It was a fact that the shiny quality cars got there early and parked on the front streets, not in the alleys.

The men were 90% farmers and concentrated around Back and Bailey Hardware and the basement barber shop. If you were looking for someone in particular, this would be the best place to find him. They talked for hours about the weather, the crops, the economy, and the government programs (in The Depression years, WPA, RFC, CCC, PWA, and many more). The economy was a topic of great concern as this was during the years 1929 to 1936. Farms were regularly being auctioned off by the banks. Banks were closing. On top of this, there had been two years of horrible drought and a plague of grasshoppers and locusts. Things could hardly get worse! And there was a lot to talk about.

The women traipsed from the dry goods store to the grocery store, looked much and bought little. A minimal existence was all they knew. The little kids tagged with Mom. Older brother or sister, when permitted walked the main street from South End to North End in company with neighbor kids. Flirtatious and sly glances were not uncommon as groups of boys met groups of girls. Since the communities of Burton, Richland Center, Reiter, Woodrow, Talma, Tiosa, Metea and Fulton, plus Rochester, were represented on Saturday nights, the boys and girls of amorous age had a broad selection. From this group evolved the group where a boy and girl walked together, albeit not too close, and finally to those who took walks into the darker side streets past nice residences. The garb was plain to say the least. Clean overalls and shirts for the boys. Sometimes they wore shoes sometimes not. For girls it was a dress of feed sack print. The shirts and dresses were sewn by Mom or an older sister. This youth parade lasted from 7:30 to 9:30pm and, if they could miss Mom or Dad's signal to come, maybe 10:00pm. Then the line of Fords, Chevys and Plymouths started up and headed for home, as the cows would be ready to be milked by 5:00am. The cars parked in front were usually loaded with Mom, Grandma and her friends. They visited in the comfort of the car and watched the greatest parade know to Moms and Dad, their Youth Parade.

I found this means of courtship occurs elsewhere when later in life my wife and I were staying at an inland town in Brazil, the town of Pocos de Caldas. Their youth parade resembled the one I had known. They walked around a park in a large circle and met face to face with girls one way and boys the other. The parents and older people were located firmly on the park benches in the center. I think Tim and Cindy took a stroll!

Back to Saturday night in Rochester. For those who had 10 cents or 15 cents, the greatest entertainment was the Char Belle Theater. You could be thrilled beyond words by movies of T. Mix, S. Temple, etc. The 10 cent price kept many walkers on the street. Another movie theater, The

Rex, competed for 5 and 10 cents. About 1934, the big ICE CREAM SHOP, all shiny and clean opened. A big cone (double dip) sold for 5 cents. This struck to the heart of the small hoard of change Mom was saving. It was our parents' wishes to let everyone spend 5 cents for ICE CREAM, which meant a total of 30 cents. That was tough as a day's work paid $1.00 and Castleman's hired hand got $5.50 per week and 3 meals. As Dad said, "If you don't have the 30 cents, we won't go to town". A mental picture yet remains of old and young crowding into the Double Dip Shop. Everyone was sitting or standing, licking cones of brown, yellow, white and red.

Social entertainment and usually handbills preceded the coming Chatauqua or Medicine Shows. These people really excited me, as their medicines seemed to take care of every illness known to man. I couldn't imagine why they had to talk so long and imploring to sell a few bottles. The Chatauqua was costly at 25 cents. I only caught glimpses from the entry tent cover, but I heard the words and stayed until Dad came and got me. Great dramas or comedies were presented by people that I felt were gifted beyond words. Chaplin and Pickford and many more started this way.

Leaving town in our 1924 Buick on one Saturday night, near 10:00pm by Dad's pocket watch, we hit the gravel at the edge of town and hurried home. The Erie Railroad had to be crossed twice and there were some perils inherent. The crossings of two tracks were on two slightly different levels, which were to be crossed slowly, but my dad usually gave us a lift as we took the jump and bump. The second crossing on the way home could be timed. You could see a train approaching and it was often an effort to outrun the train.

The Earl of Burton

This Saturday night, Dad took the first crossing with a leap and we saw a train coming from the east. He sped to Garner's corner, turned and looked for the train not yet in full view. He went westward, our backs to the tracks as the train appeared in full view. We were within a quarter mile of the crossing and the train was ½ mile away. It was inky dark so I could not tell if it was a freight or passenger train. I was 9 years old, riding in the back seat with Sister June. My mother held Baby Muriel. My mother rarely criticized my Dad's driving, but told my dad, "Earl, wait on the train". Dad replied that we were way ahead of the train and speeded up. As the road and rail distance narrowed, we were going parallel with the floodlight, which was getting bigger fast. Dad stepped on the accelerator full tilt and the Buick went fast. As we started at an angle across the tracks, the blast of whistle from the engine sounded and I watched the big engine bearing down in a real scary manner. As Dad crossed and cleared the track, the engine roared within a few feet of our rear, a fast passenger headed for Chicago. My mother cried and Dad stopped and we were all quite nervous. To me, locked in the back seat, the danger was electrifying and Sister June cried hard. Dad told Mom he'd never do that sort of thing again and he never did, so far as I know. In the years since I always shiver whenever I cross there!

CHAPTER 5

Farming Without "Earl"

The Sermonette 137

Neighbors 140

Cow in the Muck! 142

The Sermonette

My Father broke his leg one summer when his stallion fell over onto him. He also developed a series of boils and carbuncles on his legs, ankles, back and arms. Dr. Loring drove to visit him and declared him to be a sick man. He even had a fever. In 1926 there was no means to treat blood infections, so Dr. Loring prescribed herbs and concoctions. My mother despaired. He could only run the farm from his bedroom window. It was a slow process but eventually he did improve.

One day Reverend Roudebush, the minister came greeting us. He told Earl he would like a moment to chat. Earl was propped up on the couch with pillows. Mom, Baby June and I sat nearby and listened to this man.

Now the bible once came forth with a man, Job who walked in the major of the Lord. He put all work into the hours between light until dark, did good to many, honored God, had large flocks, many workers and generated a huge family who were a blessing and also followed God. He protected many of his tribe from roving enemies, engineered water to the gardens, controlled the oasis and fruited valley. The wonders of God in the desert multiplied in Job, who was a man of God.

Then all rains ceased for three or more years. The locusts came and ate. They took every living plant and laid waste to the earth. The water holes in the oasis dried up and enemies plundered the storage of food. There was no more food for his family and the tribesmen. Eventually he saw the end of the day on the desert land. He lay on a bed of fire ants and was near death when the Lord of Heaven appeared beside his bed and called "Oh Job, good and faithful servant. I need you to rise, carry on, give leadership and help to the dying and sick". The spirit helped him, giving him a new burst of energy. Over the next two years Job restored his tribe, his cellars, his water, his believers, his herbs and his body. His horses drove off the enemies and credit was accorded to God's people. Years continued under Job's guidance. Not all were followers and many marauded and even Job heard other voices at times and failed God.

Those evil hands cast new burdens on Job and his tribes. Diseases with no cure swelled the burials. Job's family was called by death. Driven winds swept the desert for years and Job yearned for the Father. He had boils and sores up and down his legs, his ankles, arms and shoulders and neck. He reeked of pus and infection. Most preferred to remain aloof from him. His body suddenly came into high heat and the death angel flew by, hovered above and called for Job to be cleansed. The pus ran off and the boils and the sores dried. Job was restored and applauded for his work ethic and love of man and God. In his time many things were righted, water flowed, new generations prospered and milk and honey were present.

Now Job again yielded his all, but prosperity brought unfaithfulness and forgetfulness of the Lord. In a few years Job was enclosed in the skin of bones and had skin lesions that tortured him. He pleaded with God for the consummation of his life. Jehovah wafted him aloft and Job now works in the inner courts of the God above.

Reverend Roudebush then prayed. He left the story with my mother and me. Mom said she thought the pastor was striking a similarity between Job and Dad, but declared my

The Earl of Burton

dad had miles and miles to go before the Lord soaked his bones up and took him off.

Note: Soon our fields of corn and crops suffered and we were sad. Our cows bellowed. One morning my mother called me and I ran out to see fifteen or more teams pulling corn plows turning into our lane. They plowed our fields and at noon the ladies of the community church fixed a lunch in the yard. We decided this was the manna from heaven. About this you can read from the <u>Neighbors</u> and about the lunch in the yard by neighborly ladies. My mother thanked them. One of them shushed her and said they would have to work all year to keep up with her husband's many favors to them. Mom cried.

A couple of weeks later Dad was on crutches and doing some chores – what he could. A neighbor fixed him a box and leg guard. He began by milking a couple cows, later half or more of them.

Neighbors

It was again the summer Dad broke his leg and it was interminably long. It was little or no joy for a boy trying to do what his father told him to do from the bedroom window. Like Murphy's Law, things usually did not go right.

Our crops were planted late and we had more weeds in them than one could believe. The weed seed in the ground had not been worked carefully and the weeds grew faster than the corn, soybeans and oats. Our efforts to plow out the weeds were unsuccessful. Lloyd and I had planted more than we could do, especially with our pains with the milk inspector and the interruptions of people bringing their mares to service. In short, we were in great trouble and without a crop we could not feed our cows and horses.

On Friday morning, June 25, Lloyd had gone to the Yellow Barn Place to plow corn with the 2-row corn plow. I had to get the milk cooled and the barn dressed up. I heard our dogs barking and came out of the barn. Bill Baldwin was driving in our lane with his single row cultivator. Not far behind was Jim Mathias with his 2-row cultivator followed by a whole line of horse drawn cultivators. Next Dee Barrier came with his black team, Clyde Earl with his 2-row plow, Ogden Marsh and Uncle Ora each with a single row. Ross Moore came on his single row, even Mose Hetzer and his white mules were there. Vernon Castleman sent his hired man with a team. Roy Anderson, who always had the cleanest cornfields, came to clean our cornfields. A 2-row corn plow came from Sand Hill Farms and finally Bill Hudkins joined the army of corn plowers. Dad came out on his crutches and talked to them and they went to

The Earl of Burton

work. Oh I was happy and felt like we were saved from disaster!

My mother was wondering how she could feed them all but Aunt Mae told her the Ladies Aid Society was fixing the meal and it would be spread under the only tree in our yard.

These good farmers saved our crops. The corn seemed to jump and the weeds never caught up. I was eternally grateful to all, even the ones that teased me.

My dad was a Do-Gooder and would have been the first to help a neighbor if they needed it. This was his time. He had tears in his eyes when I went to him at 8:30pm. I was happy for the first time this summer and I got tears in mine, too!

Cow in the Muck!

Late in August, with my father's leg slowly mending, Lloyd Reese and I struggling to keep the farm going and the milk inspector content, another crisis appeared.

One hot evening Dad had sent his dog, Bill to get the cows from our usual overnight pasture. The cows came, followed by Bill. However, Bill missed one cow. She was on the other side of the ditch. She had crowded the ditch bank and highway and was bawling. I had to go get her. Bill went along. When he saw his prey, he took over and ran to a ditch crossing, then hard at her. She got very nervous. As he moved in, she gathered herself and jumped into the ditch at the muckiest spot possible. She floundered and wiggled and dug herself completely in. Only her back, neck and head were out. I remembered that when this sort of thing had happened before, my dad had built crossings. I ran home and told him.

He had me lock the other cows in the barn lot and go get Lloyd Reese, who was still working in the fields mowing. Dad said to have him bring his big team and log chain and doubletree down to the corner of the ditch and the road. He had Mom and I help him to the car. She drove him down the road to the ditch where he could see. He was the boss. He had me bring a big hay rope when Lloyd came. Dad and Mom went to get more help from Jim Mathias and his big team. Jim was not home, but on his return, harnessed up his big team and got there about 7:00pm. Lloyd Reese and I had put the chain around her neck. We tried to dig in and put the hay rope around her front legs, but the muck filled in as fast as we shoveled it. Lloyd pulled on her neck with his team, Bill and Betty. I knew they were strong as I had

The Earl of Burton

seen them pull a stone boat in a pulling contest. They stretched the cow's neck good but couldn't move her body.

We didn't dare pull on a leg, as it would have broken or pulled it out of the socket. After Jim came with his team, about twelve more men came to help. One brought a slip scoop. They hooked Lloyd's team to it and for 1½ hours, we scooped muck away from her, exposing more of her, but still a team would not move her. The cow was in a bad way and as luck would have it, she was a good cow, giving 6 gallons of milk per day. One of our best! Her name was Ethel, after Jim Mathias' wife, where Dad had bought her.

It got dark while the men were scooping more muck using the team and scoop shovels. They finally got a hay rope around her front legs and up her back. Two teams were hitched to her neck with a hay rope. One was pointing north, the other team headed south into the pull. Both teams tightened up and stretched into their collars. The cow heaved and turned over. The horses drug her down the ditch on her back and finally out and over the bank. We were all sure Ethel was a goner. Nothing could survive such a pull, but after they unhooked and straightened her out, she gagged for air, belched, rolled her eyes and finally decided to live. By midnight she even walked home ¼ mile, although limping badly and carrying lots of mud. Dad insisted we wash her udder and milk her out a bit.

Obviously this was the best show in town and at one time or other had 30 people were watching. I was dog tired and I didn't care much about the cow. She did have a strong neck through!

Note: Muck is extremely black soil of the peat family and raises excellent crops. If it becomes to wet, as in a ditch or creek it becomes almost bottomless and can play havoc. Frank Rarick used to tell me he was going to throw my pony in the muck. If he had ever tried, he'd of had a tiger on his back!

From My Pen

Should you desire more, I'd be complimented and will forward you other stories from "My Pen"

1. A Miracle in Snow, December 25, 1944
2. A Yank Goes Abroad
3. Bob of Burton
4. Special People I've Engaged With
5. Naturally – Birds, Bears, Cows, Skunks
6. Living Abroad – Brazil and Hawaii
7. Travels over This Planet
8. Schools – As a Student and Career (55 years)
9. Dis & Dat – Lots of "Wows" here
10. Personal – Ancestors, Wife, Worship, Honors
11. Real Estate Dingers

For copies of these stories write to Bob Mathias, 18500 Highway 128, Yorkville, CA 95494

Phone: 707 895-3645

Printed in the United States
52447LVS00002B/40